Axis Stone Mysteries

CAT STREET

G. L. Keady

Published in Australia in 2024
by Big Island Publishing

Big Island Publishing
PO Box 3027, Tuross Head, 2537, NSW, Australia.
www.bigislandpublishing.au

ISBN:
E-book: 978-0-6459739-8-3
Print: 978-0-6459739-9-0

Edited by: Canon Doyle
Cover design and art: Brandon Evans-Keady

TABLE OF CONTENTS

CHAPTER
ONE

There are street kids who sleep rough, surviving on begging and theft in a city that doesn't acknowledge their existence. Why? Because the people have their own lives to worry about.

The mad dash through the Temple Street Night Market, just before closing at midnight, was, for two teenage street kids, Rai and Wing, the most important part of their day.

The name Rai is derived from a Japanese manga character. Rai didn't know his real name, but his inherited name suited him just fine; it meant lightning or thunder. As for Wing, his Chinese name means glory, but both boys knew Wing stood for his great speed because Wing could outrun almost anyone.

At closing time, the market vendors would discard their refuse; one person's rubbish is another one's treasure, and for the two boys, it was a feast for their famished stomachs.

The best source for a handout at the market were the dai pai dongs; the open-air restaurants.

This night was different. For a start, it was raining, which meant fewer people and fewer handouts. But more than that, as they were making their way through the series of dark alleyways that led to their squat under the flyover, Rai and Wing came across something sinister. A man was on his knees, head bowed, in the middle of the shadowy alleyway with his hands fastened behind his back, surrounded by three men. The boys stopped and hurriedly hid behind an industrial wheelie bin to watch. They flinched at the glint of light that reflected off the razor edge of a cleaver one of the men was holding behind his back. Then, with one quick, chilling movement, the man with the cleaver sliced it across the throat of the man on his knees, who collapsed. The boys exchanged looks of terror. Then, from behind, they heard footsteps. They turned; a fourth man was striding up the alleyway to join the others and had seen them.

In a panic, realising they'd witnessed a slaying, the boys jumped out from their hiding place and ran towards the man approaching them, expecting to easily slip past him. But, with lightning reflexes, the man caught Wing by his plait. Rai stopped, unsure what to do ... the last person he expected to get caught was Wing, seeing he was so fast. The other three men were running towards them.

Wing cried out, "Run Rai, run!"

Rai knew they weren't going to let Wing live and they'd kill him as well, so, reluctantly, he ran. As he reached the end of the alleyway, he heard Wing's screams and running footsteps coming towards him. Just then, a door opened, a hand reached out and dragged Rai inside. Someone had saved his life.

~ ~ ~

My ribs had healed, and I felt like I could outrun a racehorse. Patricia had done a fantastic job organising the office, leaving me with time on my hands. Now, you might think that's a good thing, but for a bloke like me, that spells boredom. Kendy was busy studying for her Private Investigator walk-in examination, which I must say, in NYC, was expensive—over two and a half thousand in fees. I'd been lucky; the U.S had accepted my Australian PI licence, which hadn't cost me anything like that, mainly because I'd completed three years to graduate with a Bachelor of Criminology from the University of New South Wales.

I was chilling in my office when 'The Terrible Tango' jarringly interrupted my thoughts—a mental note to myself to change that ringtone. The caller ID flashed Charlie's name. "Mr Chan, what can I do for you?"

"How are the ribs?"

"Perfectly mended, combat-ready for whatever's next. Anything up your sleeve?"

"Thought there was, but it fizzled out to nothing."

"Such is life."

"Just a heads up—I'm going off-grid for a bit ... Carmen's steering the ship while I'm in Hong Kong."

"Oh? What's the occasion?"

"Just got word my uncle passed away. His wife left us a few years ago, so now I'm the only one left to settle his affairs."

"I'm sorry to hear that. Were you two close?" I inquired.

"He was the one who got me to the U.S., to live with his brother in LA. Didn't really get to know him, but I owe him everything I've become."

"In that case, you owe him a great deal, and so do I, considering the remarkable person you've become."

"Thanks, Axis. All going well, I should be back in a week or ten days. Carmen's your go-to if you need anything."

"Keep an eye out for an office in his estate, will you? A Hong Kong outpost could be a game-changer for A, V, and C."

"Will do. Take care of things here."

"And you there. Remember, I'm just a call away if you need anything."

As I set the phone down, I couldn't help but sense the depth of emotion behind his composed facade, a clear sign of the turmoil he was experiencing.

~ ~ ~

Charlie was met at Chek Lap Kok arrivals by a trim, young lady in a tailored grey business suit, holding a piece of cardboard bearing the name Charlie Chan. She introduced herself as Wei Ling and walked Charlie to a waiting car.

After an hour's drive in traffic, Ling ushered Charlie into the Kowloon Tong low-rise apartment that belonged to his uncle. It was quaint and old-fashioned, exactly what Charlie had expected. Ling worked for Zhong Heng Lawyers, the firm handling the Ki Chan estate. She handed Charlie a dossier and left with minimal conversation.

Charlie opened the curtains and then the window, attempting to dispel the musty scent of mildew. He settled into an old armchair and opened the dossier.

Three hours later, Charlie awoke in a darkened room. Despite travelling business class, the sixteen-hour flight had left him jet-lagged. In reality, it took two hours to board the plane and another two hours to disembark, plus the sixteen-hour flight time; a total of twenty hours from which he needed to recover. However, after only a three-hour power nap, he felt rejuvenated and ready to proceed—but first, he required sustenance. He changed, took the dossier with him, and descended the four flights of stairs onto La Salle Road. A brief walk in the crisp night air led him to a modest yet appealing restaurant.

As one of the few patrons, he ordered and then settled back to peruse the dossier.

What he discovered was astonishing. He had inherited the Kowloon Tong apartment, valued at around 13 million Hong Kong dollars or 1.6 million US dollars. Additionally, there was a 60% shareholding in a nightclub called Utopia 8, 100% ownership of an office in Sheung Wan on the Hong Kong side, and an old 2009 BMW M3 Convertible. The bank accounts totalled a hundred thousand Hong Kong dollars, so he surmised he would need to liquidate these assets to settle any bills. Then, he found the death certificate. Ki Chan, aged 73, had died from blunt force trauma to the head— Charlie's uncle had been murdered!

The next morning Charlie phoned Zhong Heng Lawyers and made an appointment to meet with Mr Heng.

The lawfirsm was located at Admiralty, a mere sixteen-minute journey on the MTR from Kowloon Tong.

In the lavish office complex, Charlie was escorted to the office of Michael Wong, who specialised in wills, probate, and trusts. A pleasant, well-mannered individual in his early forties, Wong was British educated Chinese, with a receding hairline and dressed in a finely tailored suit. Speaking with a distinctive British public-school accent, he guided Charlie through the will and the associated costs of settling the estate.

"I presume you'd prefer to expedite matters, so I've prepared the most efficient plan to do so, starting with liquidating the primary asset, which is the majority shareholding in the nightclub Utopia 8."

"Yes, I saw that. Why would that be the main asset? I would have thought the Kowloon Tong property would be worth more?"

"Actually, no. The freehold of Utopia 8 is owned by the shareholders, with your late uncle holding the majority share."

"You know, I must admit, I didn't know my uncle very well. In fact, I only stayed with him for less than six months before he sent me off to his relatives in the States."

Wong leaned back in his chair, a knowing look on his face.

"Yes, we've conducted the due diligence required by law on your relationship with Mr Chan. During those six months, he and his wife applied for legal adoption, which was granted some two years after you'd left Hong Kong. As this occurred just before the handover to China, under the different laws then, your adoption was entirely legal."

"Oh, I had no idea," Charlie expressed, quite taken aback. "I also had no idea my uncle..."

"You mean your father..." Wong interjected.

"Yes, I suppose you're right. The Chans would have adopted me as their son."

"Exactly."

"I had no idea my father was involved in the nightclub business."

"Yes, he was quite the entrepreneur."

Charlie leaned forward, his gaze fixed on Wong. "Then, why was he murdered?"

Wong seemed unsettled by the intensity of Charlie's question.

"I think it best if you discuss that with the police. I can connect you with the investigating officers. For now, my role is to finalise the estate matters."

"I can't proceed without understanding what happened, you understand," Charlie said trying to lighten up.

"Well, you should know there's an existing offer to buy out your father's 60% share. It's a one-time offer from the other 40% partner, and you only have 30 days to accept."

Charlie's suspicions about Wong's motives grew.

"And why is that, Mr Wong?"

"I believe these negotiations have been ongoing for a while without a conclusion."

Charlie nodded, piecing together the puzzle.

"So, could these negotiations have led to my father's death? Are we dealing with a criminal element here?"

"I wouldn't go that far, Mr Chan. Let's just say the other party wants this resolved within the given timeframe."

Charlie stood up. "Thank you, Mr Wong. You'll hear from me." He handed Wong a business card. "My contact details, should you need to reach me."

Wong's discomfort was palpable; he was clearly unhappy with the turn of events. Charlie surmised that Wong had hoped he would swiftly agree to everything, eager to return to California. In this, Wong was mistaken.

Wong had given Charlie the details of the detective leading the murder investigation, prompting Charlie to cold call him.

The Criminal Intelligence Bureau in Wan Chai was just a short walk from Admiralty. Upon entering Arsenal House, Charlie was directed to the office of Detective Lei Peng on the 11th floor.

Detective Peng greeted Charlie at the elevator, leading him along a corridor to his modest office. Peng, in his thirties and of slighter build than Charlie, had a friendly demeanour.

"Mr Wong informed me about your visit. You are the adopted son and heir of Ki Chan."

"Yes, and I am a partner at the U.S. firm Stone, Vargas, and Chan Investigations. Is my father's murder case under your jurisdiction?"

Peng, who seemed initially unaware of Charlie's background, looked impressed.

"Yes, it is."

"Could you provide me with the details, please?"

Peng's office boasted an excellent view of Hong Kong harbour. From behind his desk, he turned his computer monitor to face Charlie, who leaned in to read the file, displayed in Chinese.

"Can you read this, Mr Chan?"

"Yes, no problem."

Charlie quickly scanned the report, surprising Peng with his speed.

"This is inconclusive ... there are no suspects. Have you thoroughly investigated my father's murder?" Charlie asked, a hint of sarcasm in his tone.

Peng appeared uncomfortable. "To be honest, Mr Chan, your father was found face-down in the alley behind Utopia 8, his nightclub. The time of death was estimated within an hour of when his body was discovered at 4 AM. He was struck from behind, presumably with a hammer, but the murder weapon wasn't found. There was no evidence at the crime scene—"

Charlie interjected sharply. "Like I said, Peng, I can read Chinese. Who found the body?"

Realising Charlie's direct approach, Peng answered succinctly. "A kitchen hand from Utopia 8."

"Have you looked into potential enemies of my father?"

"Yes." Peng scrolled through the document. Charlie noted the list of over twenty persons of interest.

"Who among these suspects seems most likely?"

"We've only scrutinized the business partners, but—" Peng hesitated.

"But what?"

"I have no solid leads. They all have alibis, and any of them could have orchestrated a hit. They're all involved in criminal activities, Mr Chan; they're Triads. As you can imagine, this makes them difficult to investigate. When you're dealing with the devil, you should expect—"

Charlie cut him off again, uninterested in platitudes. "So, the forty percent stakeholders in Utopia 8 are criminals. They wanted my father to sell his sixty percent share, and when he refused, they killed him. Is that what you're suggesting, Detective Peng?"

"That's one possibility, Mr Chan, but there could be—"

"I'd like the names and contacts of my father's partners for my own investigation."

"I can't provide those, Mr Chan. Your private investigator's license needs first to be validated in Hong Kong."

"Then, could you guide me on how to get that done?"

Peng escorted Charlie to the administrative level.

An hour later, Charlie left Arsenal House, no more informed than when he had arrived and without any investigative authority from the police. The processing of his application would take several days, and as a non-resident of Hong Kong, there was no guarantee of approval.

CHAPTER TWO

Trish and I were lounging on the sofa, engrossed in a Netflix movie, when 'The Terrible Tango' suddenly blared out. Scrambling to find the phone buried under a heap of clothes we'd shed earlier, I finally located it.

"I thought you were going to change that ringtone?" Trish remarked playfully.

"Too good a song, what can I say?" I answered, picking up the call. "Hey Charlie, how's it going? What time is it there?"

"11 AM tomorrow. Right, it's 10 PM here..." I got up, walked over to the bar, and poured myself a shot of JD. I always found international time differences confusing.

"I hope I'm not interrupting anything?" Charlie said.

I glanced down at my nudity, then at Trish's, and replied, "Not at all, mate, just watching Netflix."

"My uncle, who it turns out was my dad, was murdered..."

The revelation hit me hard. "Your father ... but..."

"I know, it's a complex story ... but right now, the police investigation is at a standstill, and I want to dig deeper ... they won't recognise my PI license here."

"Why not?"

"China's regulations ... I've applied for a local license, but as a non-resident, it's a long shot."

"What constitutes residency? Owning property?"

"I think property ownership could suffice, but that's tied up in the estate, which could take weeks to settle. I don't have that luxury."

"Setting up Stone, Vargas, and Chan locally might be faster," I suggested.

"That's an option. I'm inheriting an office in Sheung Wan."

"Perfect. Wait, Nick's got several companies in Hong Kong. We can rename one he's not using, add you as a shareholder, and we've got a local S, V, and C branch."

"That could work. I'll scope out the office and text you the details if it's viable. By the way, didn't you and Nick liaise with the Organised Crime and Triad Bureau here?"

"Yes, we collaborated on a case. Why, suspecting Triads?"

"Indeed. My father owned sixty percent of a nightclub; the rest was held by Triads. They wanted to buy him out, but he refused."

"So, they might have orchestrated the murder?"

"Highly probable."

"I'll send you Detective Inspector Shun Zhong's direct contact. He's reliable. Need me there, just say the word. I'll coordinate with Nick about the company setup."

I hung up, refreshed my drink, and poured one for Trish, joining her on the sofa.

"Charlie in trouble?" she asked.

I nodded, a wave of concern washing over me. "Yeah, it's dicey. Dealing with the Triads in Hong Kong is no small matter."

~ ~ ~

As Charlie made his way to the Admiralty MTR station to catch the subway to Central, he phoned Wong to arrange for the key to his father's office. Wong directed him to Tat Shing Art & Antique to ask for Mr Tat, who would have the key to the upstairs office. Just as he ended the call, he received my text and quickly phoned Shun Zhong to arrange a meeting at the office.

After a brief walk from Central, Charlie arrived at Upper Lascar Row and entered the short market street known as Cat Street. There, he found Tat Shing Art and entered. Mr Tat, an elderly man with a white beard and a mischievous glint in his eye, greeted him. Charlie was unsure if the look was due to his being Ki Chan's son and the new owner of the property above Tat's shop or just Mr Tat's nature—a sceptic. Nevertheless, Mr Tat was cordial, mentioning his fifty-year acquaintance with Charlie's father but expressing surprise at the existence of a son. Charlie chose not to delve into details and simply collected the keys.

The office had a separate entrance beside Tat Shing Art, with a narrow staircase leading up to it. At the top of the stairs was a landing, a security-grilled door, and then the main door. After sorting through the keys, Charlie managed to open both doors and stepped inside. The interior was entirely vacant, comprising a small reception area and two reasonably sized offices, much larger than he had anticipated.

He was alerted by footsteps ascending the wooden staircase, followed by a voice, "Hello, Mr Chan?"

Charlie welcomed Detective Zhong at the door.

"Detective, nice to meet you."

"Call me Zhong. So, is this is your future office?"

"It's rather sparse right now, but it will suffice. I was hoping for some furniture to sit and talk, but no such luck."

"No problem, I know a café just a short walk from here," Zhong suggested.

En route, Charlie briefed Zhong on his discussions with Detective Peng.

At the Elephant Grounds Café, located on the ground floor of the Hollywood Centre, they ordered and sat down to converse.

"I'm already familiar with the case, Charlie, my condolences," Zhong offered sympathetically. "As I explained to Axis, until there's clear evidence of Triad involvement, my hands are tied."

"But the partners being Triads and holding a forty percent stake seems quite indicative, doesn't it?" Charlie questioned.

"It does, but these individuals are cunning. You won't easily prove it; they have numerous business ventures, all seemingly legitimate until something goes awry. Be aware, the takeover bid makes you a potential target."

"What's your advice? Should I just sell and return home?"

"It might be the wiser choice."

"I can't just accept my father's murder and walk away..."

"Sometimes, we must rely on the law to resolve such matters."

"Do you truly believe that will happen? Detective Peng seemed to have hit a dead end."

Their discussion lasted over an hour, with Charlie steadfast in his determination to seek justice. It concluded with Zhong agreeing to assist Charlie unofficially.

~ ~ ~

Nick effortlessly transformed one of his dormant Hong Kong companies into Stone, Vargas, and Chan Investigations (Asia) Ltd., with the three of us as equal shareholders. I promptly sent Charlie the confirmation.

Charlie informed Detective Peng about the establishment of the new local corporate entity, which Peng acknowledged would accelerate the licensing process. Subsequently, Charlie reached out to a company Nick had recommended for office furnishings. He also planned to visit Utopia 8, located in Hong Kong's nightlife epicentre, Lan Kwai Fong, while he was in town. Preferring to avoid the night time bustle, he decided late afternoon was the ideal time for his visit and contacted Wong to ensure someone would be there to meet him.

Charlie had never experienced Lan Kwai Fong before. Although it was too early for its usual nocturnal vibrancy, the area was still bustling. The pedestrian-only street, lined with small, exotic restaurants and interspersed with nightclubs, exuded a unique, eccentric charm, contrasting sharply with the rest of Hong Kong's businesslike atmosphere. Even at 6 PM, the area had an undeniable party ambiance.

Standing outside Utopia 8, Charlie pondered how his uncle—no, his father—could own such a place. It contradicted the conservative image he had always held of his parents. A lifelong question about how they financed his American education suddenly became clear.

His thoughts were interrupted by a female voice. "Mr Chan? Mr Wong asked me to meet you here. I'm Laila Sing, the assistant manager of Utopia 8."

Laila, in her mid-to-late twenties, was strikingly pretty, Indian, and stylishly dressed.

"Could you give me a tour of the club, please?" Charlie requested.

"Of course," she replied, unlocking the front door.

Inside, the club was surprisingly spacious.

"I'm always amazed by the Tardis effect here," Charlie remarked.

"Yes, it's deceivingly large. We can accommodate three hundred guests. There's this main room, four private rooms, a kitchen, and a small office at the back."

"Do you operate from there?"

"I used to work from our main office on Cat Street, but not anymore."

"When did that change?" Charlie asked.

"Just a few weeks ago. Our primary office is now in Kowloon."

"And you work there?"

"No, we're completely disconnected from it now, especially since…"

"Since my father's death," Charlie completed her sentence.

Her expression revealed surprise. "Your father? Mr Ki was your father?"

"Yes, I've inherited the business."

Laila was suddenly apologetic, clearly unaware of Charlie's involvement. "I'm so sorry, Mr Chan. My sincere condolences. Your father was a lovely man. A wonderful boss."

"It's okay, Laila. You can call me Charlie. I think I've seen enough here. Could you show me where my father was found?"

"Sure."

She guided him through the kitchen to a back door that opened into a narrow alley. The outline of a body was still visible in white chalk on the ground.

"Not the best place to end one's life," Charlie murmured, kneeling beside the outline.

"The killer must have ambushed him from the kitchen. Who discovered the body?"

"It was Ravi, our chef. He found Mr Ki during his smoke break, just minutes after seeing him last."

"Why would my father have been out here at that time?"

"I don't know. It wasn't typical for him, unless he was meeting someone."

"I'd like to speak with Ravi. When will he be here?"

"He won't be, sir. He was paid off and forced to leave Hong Kong."

"By whom?"

"The new owners, sir."

"I see."

~ ~ ~

We were starting our days at the office earlier now that Trish was in charge. It could be argued that I was becoming the very character I had long avoided: home at night watching TV, enjoying a hearty breakfast, and then off to work with a routine 'hi ho, hi ho.' Just as I felt mediocrity encroaching, an unexpected case emerged, rescuing me from the mundane. Ah, the unpredictable twists of fate.

Sitting across from me was a woman in her early forties, exuding affluence with tasteful adornments and an air typical of those accustomed to wealth.

"Mrs Austin, you're in need of an investigator?"

"Yes, Mr Stone, your reputation precedes you."

"May I ask who recommended me?"

"Mr Google. Now, about my issue..." She handed me an envelope. "Please, open this."

I unfolded the envelope, extracted a card, and read aloud, "The funeral service of Mrs Charlotte Austin, to be held at St John the Evangelist Church on..."

"Yes, Mr Stone, an invitation to my own funeral. The police seem indifferent, claiming it's not a crime to send such a thing."

"I understand their stance, but it doesn't negate the unsettling nature of it. What exactly would you like me to do?"

"Find the murderer, of course."

"But no murder has been committed."

"To you, perhaps, but I see it differently, Mr Stone."

I leaned back, intrigued. The notion of investigating a murder not yet committed piqued my interest.

"Do you have any enemies, Mrs Austin?"

"Not enemies, per se, but there are two sides of my late husband's family who might prefer me dead."

"And why is that?"

"I inherited a billion dollars from him after being married for only three days."

That caught my attention even more. "And his cause of death?"

"An accident. He fell overboard during our honeymoon."

"How old was he?"

"Ninety-two."

With each revelation, the case grew more captivating. "I'll have Patricia, my PA, present you with our contract. If you agree to the terms, we'll commence our investigation, Mrs Austin."

While Mrs Austin was with Patricia, I called Kendy into my office to brief her on the case. The first step was for Kendy to profile Mrs Austin and her family to identify potential motives. It was an ideal chance for Kendy to gain hands-on experience in basic investigative techniques.

The prime suspects, I figured, would be the immediate family members who were left out of the inheritance, harbouring only bitterness. Mrs Austin had mentioned inheriting a billion dollars, prompting me to delve into profiling the late Mr Austin.

After Mrs Austin finalised the contract, Patricia escorted her to

Kendy's office to start the profiling process. However, mere minutes later, my office door flew open, and a visibly agitated Mrs Austin burst in.

"Mr Stone, I did not agree to be interrogated by a girl. I was referred to you, not the keyboardist from The Lunatic Fringe!"

It required some effort to calm her down and explain that an investigation is methodical and requires cooperation at various levels. Her impatience was evident, likely exacerbated by anxiety over the murder threat. After some discussion, she reluctantly agreed to continue working with Kendy. This episode was a clear sign of the challenging temperament of our new client.

CHAPTER THREE

I t was shaping up to be a significant day for Charlie. Restless from a night of little sleep, his first move was to shift from the old Kowloon Tong apartment to a suite at the Mandarin Oriental. More comfortable and closer to his new operational zone, the suite's expense, covered by his inheritance, wasn't a concern.

By 7 AM, Charlie was ready to leave the apartment. It hadn't been the hideout of his turbulent youth, but it was laden with memories. He paused in the lounge, fixated on a set of photographs on the mantle, particularly one with his adopted parents, taken days after they'd rescued him. The horror of that time still made his skin crawl, and the guilt over leaving Wing haunted him. "Was I ever going to forgive myself?" he thought. Reluctantly, he packed the photos into his port. They were too precious to discard, yet too painful to keep on display.

At 10:30 AM, comfortably settled in the Mandarin Oriental Hotel in Central, Charlie gazed out at the Hong Kong Harbour and phoned Nick in Manila. The conversation was about finalising the setup of their new company. Nick had everything in hand; all that was required from Charlie was his signature on a directorship memorandum, which would be delivered to his hotel later.

"So sorry to learn of your loss, Charlie," Nick offered sympathetically.

"To be honest, Nick, I didn't know them well. I only found out yesterday they were my adopted parents."

"That must have been tough," Nick responded.

Charlie felt a rare connection with Nick, sharing such personal details. He appreciated the sense of trust and friendship that was developing between them.

His next steps were to arrange meetings with the manager of Utopia 8 and his partners. However, when he tried calling Laila, he reached her voicemail, leaving him to consider the differing lifestyles of those in the nightclub industry.

~ ~ ~

It was late evening in New York, so Charlie called me for an update. Mid-conversation, he received another call, this time from Wong, his lawyer. When Charlie returned to the line, he shared disturbing news: the apartment he had just vacated had been broken into and ransacked.

"Would they have been looking for something?" I asked.

"No, nothing of value there. It's a warning from the Triads; they want me out," Charlie concluded.

I advised caution, knowing the Triads' ruthless nature from personal experience. Charlie mentioned Nick's offer to come to Hong Kong if needed.

"Keep us posted, Charlie. We might need to team up to handle this. They're hit-and-run tacticians," I warned.

"I hear you," Charlie acknowledged, understanding the gravity of the situation.

~ ~ ~

Charlie was about to leave his hotel room when his phone rang. It was Laila, returning his call. He requested a meeting with the club manager, Ryan Khan, and she promised to get back to him.

As he stepped out of the elevator into the bustling Mandarin lobby, his phone rang again. This time, it was Detective Peng.

Glancing around, Charlie spotted Peng on his phone by the concierge. They found a quiet corner in the lobby and sat across from each other at a small coffee table. Shortly after ordering coffee from an attentive waitress, they delved into conversation.

"When did you move out of Kowloon Tong, Mr Chan?"

"This morning. I needed to be on the island," Charlie replied, wary of Peng's line of questioning. "Wong must have called you to tell you I'd moved after he'd informed me about the break-in. Are you here to accuse me of that, or do you know who did it?"

Peng reassured him, "It was clear it wasn't you, Mr Chan. We're treating the incident with utmost seriousness. I believe it's connected to the murder case."

Charlie, a hint of sarcasm in his tone, said, "Oh, I thought you had given up on that."

"Not until it's solved, Mr Chan."

As they sipped their freshly served coffees, Peng expressed his concern about Charlie conducting his own investigation without official authorisation.

"I'm just making enquiries. There's no law against that, is there?"

"It's your safety that worries me," Peng stated earnestly. "Especially considering the recent break-in, which I view as a direct threat."

"Detective, it seems more sensible to question my Triad partners than me. It's hard to see who else would issue such a 'threat.'"

Peng cautioned him against making assumptions, indicating that multiple parties were interested in his father's share of Utopia 8.

Charlie, reclining with his coffee, prodded further, "It'd be easier if you shared what you know that I don't."

"You know I can't disclose that, Mr Chan," Peng replied, finishing his coffee and standing up. "This matter should be left to the police. My advice? Accept the buyout offer for your father's shares and return to Hollywood. It's safer that way."

After Peng departed, Charlie mulled over the encounter. He began to suspect collusion between Peng, Wong, and the Triad partners. His phone rang again; it was Laila, confirming a meeting with her and Ryan Khan at the Cat Street office.

Charlie was keen to see the office transformation and was pleasantly surprised as he opened the door. The makeover had exceeded his expectations; the reception area was not only modern but exuded professionalism. As he admired the main office, there was a knock at the door. It was Laila and Ryan.

Ryan's appearance was striking, as if he had just stepped off the set of a Bollywood rap musical, complete with a gold chain, sculptured hair, and hip-hop style dress. Charlie's initial impression didn't have him overly excited, but as they conversed, he began to appreciate Ryan's demeanour. It became clear that Ryan's entire persona was modelled around his job's demands, a necessary image that didn't necessarily reflect his true personality.

Laila's smile was wide as she took in the new reception area. "Wow, the reception looks amazing," she exclaimed.

In his office, Laila was equally impressed. "And this is delish," she said.

Charlie invited them to sit. "Ryan, what caused the chef to leave so abruptly?"

"I think Ravi was frightened off by someone seriously sketchy," Ryan surmised.

Charlie delved deeper. "Do you think he saw something he shouldn't have?"

"Possibly. He might know who was involved."

Charlie's questions turned towards the club's partners. "Are you concerned about the partners?"

Ryan and Laila shared a quick, cautious glance before responding.

"Not really concerned," Ryan began, "but there's more than one party interested in buying Ki's share."

"Ki didn't want to sell, though," Laila chimed in.

Charlie pondered the implications. "So, he was being pushed out?"

"Possibly. Before Ki was killed, there were some dubious types looking for him," Ryan explained.

Laila recalled a specific incident. "Remember when Ki had to call Brutus to throw that guy out? That ended in a huge fight outside."

"And then?" Charlie pressed.

"Brutus quit," Ryan revealed after a pause. "He had been Ki's bodyguard for three years. His departure made Ki an easy target."

Laila shook her head in agreement. "It was like the inevitable was bound to happen."

Charlie inquired about Brutus's whereabouts. "Nobody knows," Ryan said. "But he took a serious beating that night."

Laila added, "Brutus was no pushover. Built like Mr Universe, he never backed down from anyone."

"Do you know the names of the other buyers?"

Ryan listed them: "Chiu Chow group; Sun Yee On, the 14K that includes Wo Shing Wo. There were also some individual offers and a private meeting Ki had."

"It's clear Ki's age and tenure made the club a target," Charlie deduced.

Laila agreed to get the names of the other potential buyers from the club's records, and Ryan committed to introducing Charlie to his partners. As they left, Charlie sat back, fingers steepled under his chin, contemplating his next move in the complex web surrounding his father's legacy.

~ ~ ~

Royce Austin was a trip. The guy had been married six times and must have paid out a King's ransom in alimony over the years. He'd made all his money from a little business he'd started in New York at the end of the Second World War. The little business, named Valiant, pretty much produced the first prophylactics sold from drugstores in the US. By the time of the swinging sixties, he owned just about every other brand of condom on offer in the country. Royce sold protection without having to use a gun.

Valiant was still punching out thousands of the little sleeping bags for mice a day, making a cool fifty million a year for its shareholders. But in my book, Royce had to have been a visionary because even with all those marriages, he'd somehow managed to hang onto his majority share in the company—a company, strangely enough, that ended up contrary to history, belonging to his last wife, Charlotte Austin.

The board of directors consisted of four family members, and two executives, with Charlotte as the chairperson, wielding two votes. How the chair hadn't been bequeathed to his oldest son and managing director of the company was a mystery I needed to solve.

Before tackling it head-on in my usual fashion, I decided first to learn what Kendy had unearthed. I wandered into her office. "Hey Ken, got an update on the Austin family?"

"Park yourself in a chair because you're in for a ride," she said, raising her eyebrows. Patricia knocked and entered with coffees and croissants for morning tea. "This Austin family should be called the Addams family. In fact, they're so weird they make the Addams family seem normal."

Patricia sat down to listen, intrigued.

Kendy continued. "You obviously know Royce made his money from rubbers."

"As in what, car tyres?" Patricia posed.

"No, condoms," Kendy said with a smirk.

"Yep, just about every condom brand in America is owned by the Austin family company, Valiant," I explained.

"You're not going to tell me there are other uses for condoms?" Patricia questioned.

"Google it, there are stacks. No, more how since the business began to thrive in the sixties, the family has fought over ownership."

"Ah, succession…" Patricia said.

"Um yes, sort of, but unlike the famed TV series, this family has been like killing each other. It's no wonder dear old Charlotte has hit the panic button. Winning the highchair is like a death sentence."

"So what are we talking about here? Murder?" I queried.

"Worse than that; unexplained accidents."

"Like falling overboard on your honeymoon," I said.

"Yes, at the age of 92," Patricia added.

"Since 1967, there have been ... get this, twenty-two unexplained deaths by accident in the family ... like one every three years!"

"Okay, then where do we start, Ken?" I challenged her.

"It has to be Dallas Austin, Royce's first-born. He's the man who would be king but isn't," Kendy suggested.

~ ~ ~

Charlie received a call from Ryan, confirming a meeting with Tan Fang, CEO of Circle Three, which owned the other 40% of Utopia 8 Ltd. The meeting was set to take place at Utopia 8.

On his way to Lan Kwai Fong, Charlie called Zhong. Zhong was disturbed upon hearing about the trashed apartment. He saw it as a blatant threat from Ki's killer, warning Charlie to leave Hong Kong. Next, he feared, might be a physical attack. Charlie, undeterred, requested Zhong to check the missing persons database for Brutus Solomona and Ravi Dupré, explaining their potential insight into the case and their convenient disappearances.

Zhong's concern grew when Charlie mentioned his meeting with Tan Fang. "Be extremely cautious with Fang. He's the dragon head of Wo Shing Wo, the oldest Triad society in Hong Kong. They're dangerous and not to be underestimated."

"They've made an offer for the club, Zhong. I can't just ignore them," Charlie reasoned. "Do you think they're behind my father's murder and the break-in?"

"I wouldn't put it past them, but it's unlikely they'd be so overt. Still, don't trust them, Charlie. Be very, very careful."

CHAPTER
FOUR

By the time Charlie arrived at Utopia 8, Zhong had updates on Ravi Dupré and Brutus Solomona. Dupré had left for Cape Town two days after the murder, despite being cleared by Detective Peng and requested to stay in Hong Kong. Solomona, reported missing two days before the murder, remained a missing person. The new information only deepened the mystery.

Waiting at Utopia 8's entrance for Ryan, Charlie's mind was a whirlwind of questions. Spotting two men with a menacing look approaching, he tensed, but they passed by without incident. A sprinkle of rain began to fall as Ryan arrived.

"Just in time, looks like rain," Charlie remarked, stepping inside the club with Ryan.

"Rainy season, have to expect it. First time in Hong Kong, Mr Chan?"

"Born here, moved to LA as a teenager. First time back," Charlie responded as they entered the club's dank interior.

"I'll just turn on the aircon," Ryan said, moving away. Charlie took in the club's ambiance, noting the cleaning job. He queried Ryan about the club's closing time and the arrival of the cleaners, learning they'd changed contractors the day of the murder.

As they talked, Tan Fang entered with his bodyguard, resembling a character straight out of 'Peaky Blinders'. Fang, a mix of charisma and menace, took a cigarette from a gold case and lit it, a habit reminiscent of Tommy Shelby.

"Mr Chan junior?" Fang growled through his cigarette.

"That I am, Mr Fang," Charlie responded.

Ryan was quickly dismissed by Fang, leaving the two men under a spotlight. Fang's smoke spiralled up into the beam before diffusing into the darkness.

"You wanted to see me?" Fang said in Cantonese.

Charlie opted for English. "You've made an offer for my shares. Can we speak in English?"

Fang's response was cold. "As of now, I believe you have no shares, Mr Chan, not until the estate is settled."

Charlie cut to the chase. "I have two considerations: finding my father's murderer and evaluating offers. Let's not beat around the bush, Mr Fang."

Fang, unchanging in expression, replied while exhaling smoke through his nose, "I don't know who killed your father. It doesn't interest me. What does is the future of the business. I don't want partners, especially not Triads."

Charlie stood his ground. "Well, Mr Fang, it really isn't just about what you want. You don't have the majority share—"

Fang interrupted, "Buy me out then."

Charlie proposed a simpler solution. "How about we make this easier? I'm here to settle the estate. Once the murderer is brought to justice, I'll negotiate the sale of the shares. You'll get the first option."

Fang's departure was as dramatic as his entrance. Crushing his cigarette into the carpet, he stared down Charlie. "If you live that long, Mr Chan."

Charlie wasn't going to back down, "Are you threatening me?"

"Take it or leave it Mr Chan."

He left with his bodyguard, leaving Charlie to contemplate the threat veiled in his words.

~ ~ ~

Charlie gazed out of the big window in his hotel suite, captivated by the display of lights on and around Hong Kong harbour. The night brought a different perspective to the enigmatic city; the Star Ferry's crisscrossing, the flotilla of boats and junks in the waterway, all a hive of activity. His phone rang.

"Hey Axis..."

"How did the meeting go?" I asked.

"Some criminal psychologists believe there are five principles of crime..."

"Ah, yes, what do they call it... concurrence."

"Yes, causation, harm, legality, punishment, and attendant circumstances ... let me tell you, all these apply to the character I met tonight."

"I hear you, I've met a dragon head, and the title sure fits the personality ... Hence the infernal question; are criminals born or made?"

"This one was definitely both. For a start, he must've binged Peaky Blinders because he had Tommy Shelby down to a tee, even to puffing a cigarette and exhaling through his nostrils."

"Ha! Was he alone?"

"No, he had a silent colossus with him. Man, what do you do when a guy with unlimited power looks you in the eye and tells you if you keep doing what you're doing you're going to end up dead? Like this is the 21st Century when you have to be politically correct ... consider everyone's sensitivities ... And here's a guy threatening my life and can get away with it."

"Yes, mate, can't sue him for intimidation," I said. "You'll have to drop your own sensitivity, Charlie, these are real stakes here ... dudes like this use fear to get what they want ... it's all they've got, and it's backed up by reputation, sometimes not even recent. Look, I tell you ... I've been there ... I had a Triad hitman with a sizable reputation hellbent on killing me, ask Zhong, he knows ... if I'd believed he could do it then I was done for ... but I didn't ... you did the right thing, Charlie, you didn't react. The shit he was laying on you works both ways, remember that."

"Got you ... so where should I take it from here? My instincts tell me he didn't have my dad killed."

"One thing for sure, he wouldn't want you to sell to another Triad clan, there's the card up your sleeve. Do you have any leads?"

"I had Zhong check on the chef that found the body, he blew town a couple of days later to South Africa ... and then Ki's bodyguard, Brutus Solomona, who took a beating out front the club a couple of nights before the murder."

"So Solomona wasn't there to protect Ki, or was he just a bouncer?"

"His bodyguard."

"Sounds like a setup, there's your lead ... whoever fought with Solomona would likely be connected to the murder," I proposed.

"But Solomona has disappeared."

"Solomona, an islander, maybe Samoan ... my guess he'd be with the Samoan or New Zealand community in Hong Kong. Go to the New Zealand Consulate in there and ask about him. If Zhong says he hasn't left Hong Kong, he'd be right, he'll either be at the bottom of the harbour or laying low with his clan until the heat cools."

"I'll do that."

"Mate, you've now opened a can of worms, be super careful, work as closely as you can with Zhong, trust him and no-one else. Okay?"

"Thanks, Axis."

For Charlie, the view of Hong Kong out of the window had suddenly lost its charm and taken on a more ominous hue.

~ ~ ~

I had woken up early to call Charlie. By the time I finished, Trish had breakfast ready for me. It was a departure from my usual croissants and coffee at the office.

"I'll need to be careful with this; if you keep feeding me up, I'll end up the size of a bus," I protested jovially.

"Don't be ridiculous, you'd never fit through the door," Trish joked, heading off to change into her work clothes. Her sense of humour was one of the many things I loved about her. From the bathroom, she called out, "How did it go with Charlie?"

Leaning against the bedroom doorframe with my coffee, still in my robe, I contemplated. "I'm worried that he might be out of his depth."

Trish peeked out from the en-suite, a look of surprise on her face. "Charlie, out of his depth? I wouldn't think so. He's as cool as a cucumber. Besides, he's a Chinaman dealing with Chinamen. He's in his element. Maybe he just needs some reassurance."

"Yeah, that's what I figured."

"A bit from you is fine, but he needs Carmen. She's his stabilizer. Why isn't she with him?"

"I dunno, didn't ask."

"Want me to call her later, hon?"

"Yeah, good idea. I've got that meeting downtown with Dallas Austin, maybe by the time I get back you'll know more."

~ ~ ~

He knew he was next. Rai was under the flyover in Kowloon Tong. He and Wing were sprawled out on the floor of a squat, shirtless. An old man, resembling a wizard with his thin Fu Man Chu-like beard, was tattooing Wing's left shoulder. The method was archaic, using a six-inch doweling with a needle fastened to its end, hammered by a small mallet. The pain was intense, and Wing had a gag in his mouth to stifle his screams. Rai, also gagged, watched in horror as the shape of a dragon, the insignia of the 14K Triads, slowly emerged amidst the smeared ink on Wing's skin.

Rai's eyes snapped shut, bracing for the inevitable. Suddenly, the needle pierced his skin, and his eyes flew open in terror. Tap, tap, tap—the sharp, excruciating pain accompanied each relentless tap of the needle.

Startled awake, Charlie sat up in bed, his eyes wide with fear, his forehead glistening with sweat. This nightmare had haunted him since his childhood, a chilling reminder of a dark past he had long tried to forget. Rising unsteadily, he made his way to the bathroom, flicked on the lights, and stared into the mirror. With a trembling hand, he pulled down the left side of his nightshirt, exposing the intricate dragon tattoo that sprawled across his shoulder. It was a permanent mark of a life he had left behind—a life where he had been forcibly initiated into the 14K Triad as a boy.

Unbeknownst to Tan Fang, the fearsome dragon head of Wo Shing Wo and the oldest Triad society in Hong Kong, his business partner was a marked member of their sworn enemies, the 14K. Charlie, now caught between his haunted past and present, bore a secret that could turn deadly if Fang ever discovered his true affiliation with the 14K, his bitter rivals.

~ ~ ~

Seated in the Valiant reception, I studied the logo on the wall behind the cute receptionist. The silhouette of a knight's head in a fancy helmet made me ponder its symbolism. As I mused about what it might be like to be a receptionist for a condom company, she caught my eye and gestured towards a door while speaking through her headset. I got the hint and went through.

On the other side, a smartly-dressed young lady led me to a large boardroom on the 30th floor of the downtown Manhattan high-rise. The view from the ceiling-to-floor windows was breathtaking. The board table, capable of seating twenty, and the clinical yet classy room ambiance spoke of immense wealth.

As I stood gazing out the window, a voice broke the silence. "Mr Stone."

Turning around, I saw a good-looking man in his mid-sixties, dressed in a grey-pinstriped Armani suit with a pink shirt and a royal blue necktie. I felt underdressed in comparison.

"Call me Axis, Mr Austin."

"Please sit, coffee?"

"Yes, black and two."

He signalled a PA outside the room and then pulled up a chair at the head of the table. "So Axis, you are looking into the claim by Charlotte that she has been threatened..." he said with a voice like a radio jock.

I sat to his left as the woman who showed me in served two coffees. "Yes, I'd like to establish a few things if I may. Firstly, the validity of the threat."

"I've seen the invitation ... found it amusing in a macabre kind of way, but it seemed real enough. Look, we all get crank calls and the like. If you're asking me, I'd suggest it's nothing more than that."

The coffee was excellent. "Would you know of anyone that might hold a grudge against Mrs Austin?"

"Just about everyone in the extended Austin family."

"Hmm, because of the inheritance?"

"Absolutely. Look, Mr Stone, Axis, two things: one, my father, even at ninety-two, wouldn't have fallen overboard the yacht. He'd been sailing it for more than half a century. Secondly, it wasn't in his DNA to bequeath a single share of the company to a wife ... To that end, he'd had six previous wives, all with prenups."

"So why was there no prenup with Charlotte?"

"Therein lies the conundrum. We all believe there was."

"Okay, if I can indulge you ... who was on the yacht at the time of the accident?"

"Two members of the Austin family, Royce's grandson Joe and his sister Camille. My brother Lincoln's kids. The crew of three, and three guests, one of Charlotte's, a shady character named Rhett Avalon, and two of Royce's closest friends and company executives, Richard Wilks and Wayne Brown."

I jotted down the names. "Any of them have cause to murder Royce or threaten Charlotte?"

"Murder? No-one has suggested anything like that."

"You did say it was unlikely a yachty such as Royce would go overboard?"

"No, none of them would wish that on the old man. But any one of them would have a grievance against Charlotte, except for Avalon."

"So then you don't suspect Royce might have been helped overboard?"

"Possible, by Charlotte assisted by Avalon ... she had motive, no-one else did."

"So then if we were to assume one of the others might have suspected that and therefore sent the note to Charlotte. Maybe to blackmail her?"

"Feasible, you'd have to ask them."

"Do Messers Wilks and Brown hold office here?" I inquired.

"Yes, Richard Wilks is the CFO on this floor, and Wayne Brown is the Vice President but you'd probably find him having an extended lunch somewhere. Doesn't spend much time doing anything less important such as his job," he said with a hint of sarcasm.

"You don't have much time for Mr Brown?"

"He's pushing eighty, should've retired years ago. Wilks is younger but is also well past his use-by-date."

"And your position?"

"I'm the CEO."

"And Charlotte, I guess, is chairperson of the board with total control?"

"You got that right. Now, if you have enough to go on..."

"One last question, Mr Austin, what would you do to have the chair?"

"If you mean murdering Charlotte, yes ... but you must understand, I'd have to stand in line."

CHAPTER
FIVE

As I was being led to the office of Richard Wilks, CFO of Valiant, I phoned Kendy. "Kendy, I'm still at Valiant. Listen, get Bulldog to check out Rhett Avalon for any form. Okay, I'll be at the office in an hour or so."

I followed my guide to a set of double doors she ushered me through. Inside was a plush reception area with a cute blonde behind the desk. Before I could even think of flirting, a door opened and a tall, good-looking man in his early to mid-sixties, smartly dressed in a suit, welcomed me into his office.

"Mr Stone, pleased to meet you. Please take a seat. How can I be of help?" he greeted me with a professional smile.

I took a seat across from him in his opulent office. "Mr Wilks..."

"Call me Dicky, Axis."

I chuckled internally at the irony of a guy named Dicky working for a condom company. "Dicky, I have a couple of questions. Firstly, why was there no prenup with Charlotte when it was standard with Royce's other wives?"

"There was a prenup, but it wasn't signed by Mrs Austin. It was supposed to be routine, but their marriage was anything but. They were married spontaneously on-board Raincoat, Royce's yacht. It caught everyone off guard."

"Where was it heading?"

"To Cape Cod. But it was more about the journey than the

destination with Royce."

Dicky narrated the yacht's departure, describing how he helped a drunken Wayne onto Raincoat. Captain Jackson had greeted them, and Wayne was quickly escorted to his cabin.

"Then I was introduced to Charlotte's friend, Rhett Avalon. He was in his late thirties, looked like a tennis coach, and I suspect he was more than just a friend to her. Royce's grandkids, Joe and Camille, were there too, both in their early twenties and quite disagreeable."

"We were an hour out when Royce announced their marriage. It shocked everyone. Wayne scrambled for a drink, and I was speechless. The grandkids openly disapproved."

"After the ceremony, I led Wayne to his cabin, and the others went up on deck. The weather was good, the waters calm. Then I heard a scream."

"Where were you?"

"In the galley. I went to the deck and found Charlotte crying in Avalon's arms, Camille in shock with a bloody nose."

"Avalon claimed Royce was at the stern one moment, gone the next. They only found his captain's hat in the wake."

"So, no-one saw him fall?"

"No. It's peculiar. Royce was an experienced sailor, unlikely to just fall overboard."

"What if he'd had a heart attack or stroke?"

"Possible, but you'd expect some sound, something."

"So, the wedding's spontaneity explains the missing prenup?" I posed.

"Seems so. But it's out of character for Royce."

"Your guess?"

"Perhaps Charlotte spiked his drink, then coerced him into marrying her on the spot, threatening to leave with Avalon otherwise."

"That would explain the prenup situation."

"Right. And then something happened on deck. Camille caught

Charlotte and Avalon in the act, or maybe she stumbled onto a plot to murder Royce."

I stood, looking out at the Hudson, deep in thought. Turning back to Dicky, I said, "Thank you, Dicky, you've been more than helpful."

"Let me know if I can assist further," Dicky said, handing me his business card on top of a box. "It's a family pack of rainbow condoms, on the house."

I liked Dicky, he had a colourful character, I guess that comes from knowing all the ins and outs of running a condom company, no pun intended.

With my next step being an interview with Miss Camille Austin, I instructed Patricia to set up an appointment. Meanwhile, Kendy signalled me into her office with an air of excitement.

"Three things," she began, brimming with enthusiasm. "First, Bulldog dug up info on Rhett Avalon, or should I say, Conway Stevens, among about four other names. He's got charges under all his aliases but none as Avalon. Born Tarak Abbas in Lebanon, he's somehow in the country despite being on the international terrorist list."

This revelation made me sit down, reassessing the entire case. "This throws everything into a whole new light. What are we dealing with here?"

"Who is he in connection to the case?" Kendy asked.

"Avalon was with Charlotte Austin on the yacht. The CFO of Valiant, Richard Wilks, who was also on board, said Avalon looks like a Hollywood tennis coach and appeared to be more than a just friend to Charlotte ... so Charlotte's latest squeeze is a wanted terrorist," I mused.

Patricia popped her head in. "I got you an appointment with Camille Austin, 'The Crow', this afternoon at her Manhattan apartment. She's off to Europe otherwise."

"The Crow?" Kendy echoed.

Patricia nodded. "Seriously poor phone manners big chance that won't change when you meet her. She'll see you at 3 PM."

"Thanks, Trish. Lock it in," I said. "Kendy, what's the second thing?"

"The band wants to record 'The Terrible Tango'," she announced.

"Fantastic news," I replied. "And the third?"

She hesitated slightly. "My PI studies asked what's most intriguing about being a PI. What do you think?"

I pondered for a moment. "Hmm, at any one time on a case like this I could be talking one on one with a murderer."

"Wow! or a terrorist even!" Kendy added, her eyes wide.

"Exactly."

~ ~ ~

Charlie was jolted awake by the ringing of his cellphone. Fumbling for it, he checked the time—just after midnight.

"Hello, who is this?" he asked, groggily irritated.

"It's Brutus Solomona, Mr Khan gave me your number."

Immediately alert, Charlie sat bolt upright. This could be the breakthrough he needed. "Sorry for the attitude, Brutus. I was asleep."

"I didn't mean to wake you. I guess I'm a night person."

"Brutus, I need to talk to you."

"Okay, but not over the phone. You get that, right?"

"Yes. Where and when?"

"Where are you now?"

"The Mandarin Oriental Hotel."

"Meet me outside the back door of Utopia 8 in an hour. Can you do that?"

"Yes, I'll be there. See you then."

"Come alone and don't tell anyone about this meeting. That includes Mr Khan."

Charlie knew he had to slip into Utopia 8 unnoticed. If necessary, he'd find a way around to the back of the club and the alleyway. When he arrived, he realised entering incognito wouldn't be an issue—the club was bustling and vibrant, filled to the brim with people.

Navigating through the crowded room, he moved to the rhythm of the loud, thumping nu-disco music, orchestrated by a DJ on a small stage at the back. Charlie tried to blend in, but in a sea of revellers, he felt conspicuous.

After a tense dash through the busy kitchen, he reached the back door. His heart raced at 130 bpm, syncing with the music. He opened the door and stepped out. Instantly, the light went out and music faded into a distant blur, replaced by the shrill sound of tinnitus.

Way in the distance, Charlie could faintly hear a voice screaming, "Run Rai, run!" He jolted awake with a start.

"Take it easy, Mr Chan," a soothing voice said.

Confused and disoriented, Charlie's vision slowly came into focus. He saw three people hovering over him. He recognised Ryan and Laila, but the third person was unfamiliar. They helped him to his feet. When he touched the back of his head, his hand came away with blood.

"What the hell happened?" he asked, bewildered.

"Someone hit you," Ryan explained.

"You're lucky Deni was coming out for a smoke. He scared them off. They might have killed you," Laila added.

Deni, the new chef, a big Chinaman with a broad face, smiled at Charlie, revealing a gold front tooth. "Thank you, Deni," Charlie muttered. "How many were there, Deni? Did you get a good look at them?" he asked.

"Three with nunchucku. I got meat cleaver," Deni chuckled proudly. "No contest. I not recognise them, I'm new here ... Triads, I think," he said in broken English.

"Thank goodness for you, Deni. What happened to Brutus?" Charlie mumbled, trying to piece things together.

"Brutus? Did you speak with him?" Ryan interjected.

"Yes, you gave him my number. I was here to meet him."

"I didn't give Brutus your number. I haven't heard from him at all."

Realisation struck Charlie like a wave. He had been set up. "They must have Brutus captive. I know it was his voice on the phone. He had a Samoan accent."

For Charlie, the situation had just taken a more complicated turn.

~ ~ ~

I looked up at the Flatiron Building on Fifth Avenue, the most coveted address in Manhattan, aware that Camille's 12A apartment would have cost her at least twelve million and change.

Breezing through security, I pressed the button at the double doors. After a moment, the doors opened to reveal a young woman clad in a tracksuit, headband, and runners, appearing as if she had just returned from a jog—or more likely, stepped off a treadmill. Silently, she stepped aside, allowing me entrance, eyeing me as though I were an unappealing dish on a menu. A gesture of her hand directed me to the white suede lounge in the expansive living room. The view from the massive floor-to-ceiling windows was breathtaking. I initiated the conversation.

"Miss Austin, thank you for giving me your time."

"Yes, well, use it wisely, I'm not giving you much."

Her tone was as sharp as a crow's caw.

"I'm a private detective representing Mrs Austin."

"Don't tell me your problems," she retorted sarcastically.

"I'd like to ask you a few questions about the night of the accident."

"I've already provided enough for the memoirs, why don't you just read the police report?"

She crossed her legs and smirked at me. Observing her, I noted her body was slender, small-breasted but well-proportioned, her petite figure squeezed into a tight tracksuit—I was reminded of Olivia Newton John in her video of the hit song 'Physical'.

"There are questions outside of what the police—"

She cut in, "Go on then…"

"How did you get the nosebleed?"

"That sketchy Avalon gave me a backhander."

"Why?"

"Because I accused him of sleeping with Charlotte, that's why."

"How did you know that?"

"Der, do you think I'm stupid? … While Pop was busy falling off the stern of Raincoat, they were too busy to notice."

"Why?"

"They were getting it on."

"Having sex?"

"I caught her giving him head."

"So, was Royce already overboard when you caught them?"

"Hard to say. I didn't notice him when I went up on deck. It wasn't until Joe saw his hat in the water."

"Joe, your brother … he was already there?"

"We were both below; I went to top up my champagne at the bar and he went up to join Pop and Charlotte. I didn't realise Avalon would be there. I caught them, threw my champagne over him and he slapped me."

"What did Joe see?"

"I don't know. We didn't talk about it."

"Are you on good terms with your brother?"

"No. We don't talk."

"Why were you and Joe invited on board?"

"Never found out, but Pop mentioned it was something important. Had I known Joe would be there, I wouldn't have gone. Talk to him if you want to know more. Look, I'm not interested in helping that bitch. She ensnared the old man and stole the family fortune … I think you get the picture." She stood up, signalling the end of our meeting.

"Thank you for your time," I said.

"It would be better spent catching those two for plotting Pop's murder and robbing the family. Goodbye, Stone."

Back down from the ivory tower, amidst the common folk in the street, I felt more at ease. Yet, I couldn't help but ponder how someone like Camille, endowed with immense wealth, could possess such scant empathy and be so egregiously obnoxious. She acted way too old for her age. My investigation was now steering me towards Joe Austin, with Rhett Avalon emerging as the prime suspect in the murder of Royce. However, implicating Avalon could potentially involve my client, and my mandate wasn't to probe the accident, but to identify the sender of the poison pen letter sent to Charlotte and put an end to their actions.

CHAPTER
SIX

Exiting the Sunset office, Carmen answered her cellphone. Upon learning of Charlie's ordeal, she swiftly returned to her desk and slumped into her chair, visibly shaken.

"No, no, you listen to me ... you're one step out, Charlie. Sooner or later they're going to catch you. If it hadn't been for the chef..."

"I know, I know..." Charlie repeated worriedly.

"Where are you now?"

"Back at the Mandarin, it's 3 AM here. Just wanted to hear your voice."

"Why are you insisting on doing this alone, Charlie?"

"I didn't think it would come to this," he lied, his words masking an attempt to conceal his disgraceful past.

"I think you should tell Axis."

"He's got enough on his plate."

"What about Nick, then?"

"I, I..."

"Do you want me to talk to him?" Carmen offered, sensing Charlie's discomfort.

"He did offer to come here..."

"Charlie, I know you ... you have secrets you're trying to hide ... I've seen the 14K dragon tattoo on your shoulder ... I understand you want to bury your past ... but it's time to confront it, darling. Nick understands the culture; he will respect your situation."

"You're right, as usual … Call him in four hours. For now, I need to rest."

Charlie, sipping his morning coffee while taking in the harbour view, wasn't surprised when the reception called to inform him of a guest. He expected Nick Vargas, and sure enough, when he opened the door, there stood Nick.

After settling Nick's port in the second bedroom, they headed down to the Clipper Lounge for breakfast. Nick casually shared that he'd flown from Manila in his newly acquired SyberJet SJ30, the fastest long-range light jet in the world, once owned by Morgan Freeman. The flight took just an hour and 15 minutes, though Nick joked that getting out of Chek Lap Kok airport to the Mandarin almost took as long.

While Charlie was impressed by the jet, he was more taken by the effort Nick had made to support him.

Charlie briefed Nick on everything, including his teenage years, his ties to the 14K, the tragic killing of his friend, and the lengths his adopted parents went to secure his future. He spoke in Cantonese, finding it easier to express this deeply personal and confessional story. After a couple of coffees, Nick was fully up to speed.

Nick switched to English, "Carmen gave me just a basic brief. When Axis and I dealt with the Sun Yee On dragon head here, we would've been in deep trouble if it hadn't been for detective inspector Zhong from the Organised Crime and Triad Bureau."

"I've been in touch with Zhong, but he can't officially help until a Triad link is established. In the meantime, Detective Peng from homicide is on the case, but I don't trust him. Zhong's agreed to assist unofficially for now."

Nick leaned back, pondering, then leaned forward with a conclusion. "Okay, let me summarize … Brutus is beaten up, perhaps captured, to clear the path for the killers to get to Ki. They lure you to the club to take you out. You don't think it's the work of your partners, the Circle Three, a cover for the Wo Shing Wo Triad. If Fang threatened you, why don't you think he killed Ki and attacked you? What if he knows about your 14K mark?"

"It's possible, but I didn't get that impression from Fang. I think his threat was general. He's probably more worried about another Triad clan getting the Utopia 8 controlling shares."

Nick nodded, "Good deduction. If Fang wanted you dead, it would've been done already. But he's in a tight spot. He can't act until you officially own the shares. And even then, he'd need to know who you'd leave them to."

"Exactly, Nick. I don't think Fang killed Ki. But he didn't expect me as the heir—that was my parents' secret."

"So Fang's motive was likely thinking there was no heir to Ki's shares. But not to kill you. It's typical Triad tactics—using fear to push you to sell."

"Right. So, what's the play?"

"Do you want the club?"

"No."

"Then appoint someone on a commission to gather all offers. It keeps you safe and reveals the players. Most importantly, what's your priority—selling Utopia 8 or solving Ki's murder?"

"Solving the murder."

"Then we focus on rescuing Brutus. He's key. Zhong will help because it's not in Detective Peng's hands and likely involves the Triads."

"Should I have Michael Wong from Zhong Heng Lawyers handle the offers?"

"Yes, but ensure they sign a non-collusion agreement to prevent corruption."

Charlie slapped Nick's knee, appreciative. "It's fantastic to have you and Axis as partners. Now, let's head to our new Cat Street offices."

~ ~ ~

I was surprised to find Charlotte Austin waiting for me at the office.

"Charlotte, are you here to see me or—?"

"You, we need to talk."

Patricia shot me a 'she's in a crappy mood' look, and I returned it with a wink.

Trish reported, "Kendy will be back in an hour; she's at day-care."

I ushered Charlotte into my office, sensing her smouldering anger. We took seats. "What seems to be the problem? You look like you want to burn down the building," I quipped.

"I retained you to find the sender of the threat, not to investigate my husband's unfortunate death," she snapped.

"When you retain Stone, Vargas, and Chan, you accept our methodology; it's in the agreement you signed. I believe the two things are linked; solving one will lead to the conclusion of the other."

"Are you suggesting foul play in Royce's death?"

"Yes."

"Ridiculous, we were all on deck, and none of us threw him overboard."

"Best let me determine that."

"No, there is a sizable life insurance claim about to be settled, plus any further delays to the inheritance being settled will cause me stress ... The police and coroner accepted accidental death by drowning, why can't you?"

"Because of the threat to your life. Are you aware of the number of accidental deaths in this family? One every three years since Valiant was incorporated. That's extraordinary."

She calmed down slightly. "No, I didn't know that."

"Look, the inheritance will be of no use to you if you're dead, will it?"

She responded with pursed lips and a shrug of her shoulders.

There was a knock at the door. "Come in," I invited.

Patricia popped her head in and said, "I can get a meeting for you with Joe Austin at 6 PM. He's requesting the location to be The Knickerbocker Club, heard of it?"

Charlotte replied, "Only the most exclusive men's club in New

York, in the US actually. Trust him to be a member," she remarked facetiously.

"Okay, thanks, Trish, lock it in."

Trish ducked back out.

"How long have you two been an item?" Charlotte inquired smugly.

I chose not to respond to her question.

"So, my line of inquiry has shifted from Camille to Joe, in the hope that he will have witnessed something to explain how an old sea dog like Royce could fall over the stern railing and drown."

"Good luck with that; you do realise he's a bigger asshole than his sister?"

"That would be quite an achievement. Next, I have a question about Conway Stevens."

"Never heard of him."

"Look, Mrs Austin, you drop the attitude, or I drop the case. What's it going to be?"

She paused, then reluctantly agreed, "Okay, okay, sorry ... I don't know that name."

"Okay, I'll give you their other alias of his: Rhett Avalon."

"What?"

Her shock seemed genuine.

"Conway Stevens has a rap sheet as long as your arm, and he or your Mr Avalon, was born in Lebanon as Tarak Abbas, who is a wanted terrorist. "

Her previous attitude completely dissolved, replaced by concern.

"Avalon is my prime suspect, Mrs Austin." I let that sink in before continuing, "So, what can you tell me about your relationship with him?"

She sighed. "We met last year at the Beverly Hills Tennis Club and hit it off as friends."

"Just friends?"

"Well, it evolved, and yes, we became lovers. But once I met Royce, I ended it. In fact, I ended it the day we were married; that's why he was invited onboard the Raincoat."

"I don't get it..."

"He came to New York uninvited, arrived the day of my marriage. I admitted to Royce about our affair, and in his typical fashion, he wanted him on the cruise to get the message and witness us married. He thought the display of sheer wealth and power would deter any further advances from him."

"Did it?"

"I don't know. I haven't seen him since."

"So was Camille mistaken in claiming to have seen you giving him oral sex on deck that night?"

"Huh! Definitely. She said that? What a bitch."

"Then why did Avalon give her a bloody nose?"

"He didn't."

"Then who did?"

"Her brother."

"Why?"

"I have no idea."

"Do you recall anyone else on deck that night?"

"Sure, that's why Camille's claim is ludicrous; the captain was at the helm talking with Wayne Brown."

"So, why was Royce at the stern?"

"He was letting me say goodbye to Rhett."

"Okay, then why didn't anyone see what happened to Royce?"

"I think about that all the time; it just doesn't add up," she admitted.

I checked the time. "I need to take a look at Raincoat before I meet with Joe. Can you arrange that?"

"Yes." She dialled Captain Edwards.

Two hours later, I was doing what I hate most: boarding a boat. The Raincoat, moored at Pier 25 in the Hudson, looked impressive as far as yachts go. I was greeted on the companionway by Captain Edwards, a tall, amiable fellow whose appearance and demeanour left no doubt he was a ship's captain. Eager to recreate the scene from the night Royce went overboard, I asked Edwards for assistance, which he readily provided.

"It was fair weather sailing, a slight helpful south breeze, if I remember. I was here at the helm chatting with Mr Brown, while Mrs Austin and Mr Avalon were standing by the mainmast talking. Mr Royce Austin was leaning against the stern rail, talking to Mr Austin Jr., and Miss Austin."

"Camille?"

"Yes."

I positioned myself behind the helm in the captain's spot. "So, Royce was behind you. Were the brother and sister still there when Royce went over?"

"I can't say for sure, as I had my back to them. But I do remember Miss Camille made her way to Mrs Austin, because as she did, Joe Austin cried out."

"What did he say?"

"No, I think, yes, he cried out 'no.' I rushed to him and we saw Mr Austin's captain's hat floating in the wake."

"What do you suppose happened? How could a sailor of Royce's experience go over?"

"You know, the answer to that totally eludes me. I've sailed with Mr Austin for twenty years; irrespective of his age, he was a competent sailor."

"Just for interest, how far would you say Camille had made it from the stern to the mainmast before Joe cried out?"

"Not far, because I noticed her stop. Then, instead of going to Joe, as you'd expect, she proceeded to Mrs Austin. I thought that was odd."

"Hmm," I pondered. "So do I, Captain. So do I."

Captain Edwards accompanied me back along Pier 25 to my car. I shook his hand, but just before getting in, I asked, "Captain, did you pick up on the mood of everyone on deck that night?"

"You mean Mrs Austin and Mr Avalon?"

"Yes, and the other three as well."

He pondered for a moment. "I'd say the discussion between Mrs Austin and Mr Avalon was intense. As for the others, at one point, Royce's voice caught my attention because he was quite upset."

"Angry?"

"Yes, let me tell ya, the entire world it knew when Royce lost his temper ... and Mr Brown commented to me, 'The old man's pissed.' But before I could catch any more, Mr Brown requested to steer, which meant I had to disconnect the autopilot, and that distracted me."

"Thank you, Captain, you've been very helpful."

CHAPTER
SEVEN

On the way to Cat Street, Nick phoned Zhong, who was free and agreed to meet them there.

Upon entering the office, Nick immediately expressed his admiration to Charlie. The reception desk showcased the steel-scripted logo of S,V&C Investigations against a grey backdrop, a sight Charlie was also seeing for the first time.

"Carmen sent the logo design to your friends at Makeover Plus. They do great work. It's way better than the one we had made for our office in LA," Charlie commented.

"I'll get them to do one for Manila as well. It looks terrific," Nick replied.

Just then, Zhong arrived, joining them with a greeting, "Mr Vargas, the office has taken shape since I last saw it. Let's see, S,V&C ... Stone, Vargas and Chan, excellent."

"Rock 'n roll," Nick replied, shaking Zhong's hand.

"Come in," Charlie invited, leading them into his office, where they settled in the lounge area.

Nick updated Zhong on their earlier discussion, especially about Brutus. Zhong found the information compelling.

"Yes, that will definitely bring me into the case in an official capacity ... well thought through. We now need to brainstorm how to locate Brutus and then rescue him. However, I must caution you that if the triads holding him get wind of my involvement, we'll be recovering pieces of Brutus from Hong Kong harbour in no time flat," Zhong warned.

Nick and Charlie shared a look of grave concern.

A knock at the door interrupted them. Charlie answered it and returned, perusing a folder.

"It's the non-collusion agreement from Zhong Heng for me to sign. Want to look it over, Nick? The courier is waiting," he said.

Nick took the folder, reading the three-page agreement.

"Who are you dealing with at Zhong Heng?" Zhong inquired.

"Michael Wong," Charlie replied.

Zhong's expression turned sour.

"Something wrong?" Charlie asked, noting Zhong's reaction.

"Let's just say we were on opposite sides in court once," Zhong revealed.

Nick, still reading, asked, "Who were you prosecuting?"

"Sun Yee On, you remember Lee Kok Lung, don't you?" Zhong responded.

Nick looked up, "How could I forget him? That was the case Axis and I worked on with you. I think Axis might have mentioned it to you Charlie."

"Was that the Triad hitman from here Axis had to take on in Sydney in the Shark Arm Case?" Charlie inquired.

"You bet it was," Zhong confirmed. "I tell you, Axis did extremely well to defeat him. Never underestimate Mr Axis Stone."

"The agreement looks fine, Charlie, you can sign," Nick concluded. "So if you were on the opposite side to Michael Wong, then he was representing the Dragon Head of Sun Yee On, Lee Kok Lung."

"Correct, which begs the question, how can you possibly trust Michael Wong?"

Nick handed Charlie the document to sign. Charlie took it, his expression turning glum, knowing Zhong was right.

~ ~ ~

Upon arriving at the Knickerbocker Club on East 62nd Street, famous for its establishment in 1871 as a gentlemen's club with notable members like Douglas Fairbanks, JP Morgan, and US President Franklin D. Roosevelt, I was struck by its 'men only' policy, a curious anachronism in today's world focused on gender equality. Yet, the club maintained a Women's Dining Room, aside from its known code of secrecy.

I was met inside by a Boris Karloff lookalike in a dinner suit and white gloves, who evidently expected me. He guided me through a grand, vacant hall reminiscent of aristocracy, across a checkerboard floor to a spiralling staircase. At the top of the red-carpeted stairs, a pair of large mahogany doors greeted me. Stepping through, I entered a scene straight from the 19th century, half expecting Sherlock Holmes and Watson in the leather armchairs. Instead, I found only one person in a room filled with at least twenty chairs. Approaching him, I wasn't disappointed to find Joe Austin.

"Mr Stone, take a seat," the man, in his early twenties, said with a resonant voice. "Joseph Austin. You've met my sister, now I guess you wish to interrogate me."

As I sat, a waitress resembling Cloris Leachman's Frau Blucher from 'Young Frankenstein' appeared, standing over us with a stern glare. Her sudden arrival momentarily unnerved me, reminding me of movie archetypes from the films I'd been watching with Patricia.

Austin smirked at my reaction. "Order whatever you wish," he offered congenially.

I ordered a JD on the rocks.

After detailing my commission from Mrs Austin and some details of my investigation, I proceeded with my memorised questions.

"On the night Royce went overboard, Captain Edwards told me you and your sister were having an argument at the stern. Is that correct?"

"You've met my sister, just having a conversation with her is an argument, Mr Stone."

"Yes, I did notice she's rarely agreeable."

"But essentially, yes, we were having a disagreement."

"Can I ask about what?"

"Both of us want a seat on the board of Valiant, we thought we had been invited on board to discuss it but when she brought it up with Royce, well, he blew up."

"Why?"

"He said, now how did he put it, yes, 'you bask in the shade of my fortune' and therefore we weren't worthy of such an influential position. He said we needed to earn it."

"And Camille reacted to that?"

"Yes, she mouthed off about him being past his use-by-date, surrounded by old farts like Wayne Brown and Dicky Wilks … you know, yes-men. She said it was time for change. What she was really pissed over was there has never been a female on the board … and being a feminist, it was her aim to rectify that."

"Do you agree with her?"

"No, I couldn't give a crap. I know I'm in the will … the shares I will inherit will do me fine, especially when Valiant goes public."

"Oh, is that on the cards?"

"Only now the old man's gone. He adamantly resisted going public since it became a success."

"Who's driving the public listing?"

"Wayne Brown."

"I presumed he's as I've been told, an old yes-man boozer?"

"Ha, far from it, he's the marketing genius behind the success of Valiant. The old boy had the idea but Browny marketed the hell out of it."

My perception of Mr Brown had now shifted, opening a new angle of inquiry.

"Okay, so during the argument, Camille stormed off?"

"When the old boy told her that over his dead body the company will go public, and that there will indeed be a woman on the board soon enough, and that it will be Charlotte, not her, well, Camille imploded."

"And what happened?"

"She grabbed the old feller by the shirt front and got in his face, enraged like I've personally witnessed plenty of times before, I tell you, it's seriously ugly. But old Royce had never seen it before and was shocked. When she called Charlotte a gold digger or something to that effect, he slapped her one. That's what caused her to storm off … I expected to go and pay out on Charlotte."

"Then what happened?"

"I went after her."

"Wait, so you weren't with Royce when he went over?"

"No. I'd only taken a few steps, Browny had come down from the helm and Royce had gone."

"How?"

"I think after he slapped her, he either had a heart attack and fell over the railing or just staggered backward and went over."

"Wouldn't Brown have seen it?"

"You'd have to ask him, he never mentioned that he had."

I realised then, after what Joe had admitted, that it was very convenient for Brown that Royce had died. Now he could float the company … all their shares would be worth a fortune. All he'd have to do would be to convince Charlotte to agree to the public float … unless he already had. Next port of call; Wayne Brown.

Upon my return to the office, I immediately had Patricia check the companies register to determine the shareholding of the privately-owned Valiant Industries LLC. She quickly brought back the information: the main governing shareholder was company president Royce Austin with 51%, vice president Wayne Brown with 25%, CEO Dallas Austin with 15%, and CFO Richard Wilks holding the remaining 9%.

"You'd expect Charlotte would inherit a major chunk of Royce's 51 percent, with some of it going to other family members. That's where Joe and Camille come into play," I said.

"Would a few percent be enough to make them rich once it goes public?"

"Yes. They'd become millionaires, and they must already be receiving a sizeable income from the company, otherwise how could they afford their current lifestyles."

"I'd say Camille's apartment is probably owned by the company," Patricia suggested.

"Yes, and it probably pays for Joe's membership at the Knickerbockers, and picks up his tab. This gives them all motive to bump off the old feller, and a couple of them motive to threaten Charlotte."

"So, who's your money on, Sherlock?" Patricia teased, giving me a playful peck on the cheek.

"I'll reserve judgment until after I speak with Wayne Brown, but at this stage, I think I can rule out Rhett Avalon. He wouldn't gain anything, unless he's threatening to blackmail Charlotte now he knows what she'll be worth."

"Maybe she's already married or something?"

"Trish, you're a genius. Can you do some research on that? Oh, where's Kendy?" I asked.

"She came back while you were out; now she's at band rehearsals. Need her?"

"No, we can handle it. I wonder how Charlie's getting on?"

"Oh, I spoke with Carmen. Nick joined Charlie in Hong Kong to give him a hand. The office is set up now in Cat Street."

"Cool."

~ ~ ~

Nick and Charlie were strolling through Admiralty, heading towards the Mandarin in Central.

"We can use your lawyer Wong to gather the offers, knowing he'll probably favour Sun Yee On, given his apparent ties," Nick said.

"It's hard to say if he's connected, after all, he's a lawyer in a large firm, and they don't often have a choice of who they represent."

"That's true, but for now, we can't afford to give him the benefit of the doubt."

"I agree," Charlie said, just as his phone rang. "Hello? Yes, Laila, okay, we're on our way there now ... oh, myself and my partner Nick Vargas. We're walking, so we'll be there in ten minutes."

Enjoying the lovely day, they quickened their pace to meet Laila.

They found her in the lobby, looking more attractive than usual, dressed differently than her usual work attire. After introducing Nick, they settled at a table in the Clipper Lounge and ordered morning tea.

"So, you seem a bit worried. What's the problem?" Charlie asked.

"Circle Three rang Ryan and myself this morning to say we were fired," she said regretfully. "We're not asking you to do anything about it, just wanted to let you know."

"They're cleaning out Ki's staff," Charlie noted grumpily.

"Do they have that right?" Nick inquired.

"Only until I officially take control," Charlie responded.

"Oh, I see. It's about the inheritance," Nick realised.

Laila started to tear up. Nick took her hand, "Are you worried about not having a job to go to?"

She sniffled, "Yes, I live alone in Sheung Wan, and the rent is high."

"What about Ryan?" Charlie asked.

"He's okay; he lives with his family, and they're well-off. He also had an offer from a club in Wan Chai. But I don't know what to do."

"We could use a PA at Cat Street, couldn't we, Charlie?" Nick suggested cheerfully, trying to lift Laila's spirits.

"I'm not sure," Charlie replied thoughtfully, "we need one immediately, like starting right now ... and I'm not certain if Laila would be ready to start an entirely new career."

Her smile broke through her tears, touched by their consideration. "Oh, thank you. You're so kind."

"Kind? No, we need a smart young lady who would be willing not only to run the office and assist with our investigations but also to study for a local private investigator licence."

Laila looked at Nick and Charlie, wide-eyed, then said excitedly,

"Where do I sign up?"

"You already have," Nick said with a broad grin.

~ ~ ~

I had just finished arranging a meeting with Wayne Brown when Patricia entered, her expression indicating she had news to share.

"Kendy wants you to drop by the recording studio; she's got something..."

"Couldn't she just tell you over the phone?"

"No, she didn't have time; they're recording some new tracks. I got her working on researching Charlotte's background, as well as myself. I found nothing, though, must be that."

"Okay, I'll swing by on my way to meet Wayne Brown at Valiant. He said he can only spare me five minutes."

Twenty minutes later, I found myself in the control room of Village Recording Studio. I was with the engineer and Lunatic Fringe's band manager, Devon Steel, peering through the large window into the studio. The band was about to record a take of their new song, 'Last Taste'. I had heard snippets of the song from Kendy in the office, so it was somewhat familiar—a sultry ballad about lost love. Settling back, I was eager to see how it had all come together. The engineer, Ricky, dimmed the lighting to set the mood. This take was for the rhythm section, with Rag Doll providing a guide vocal. Ricky counted the band in through the talkback. The song started with Kendy on keyboards and Bla, or Zola as I preferred to call her, on fretless bass. Slick followed on smooth guitar, then Butch joined in on the kit, playing with brushes. Rag Doll, immersed in the mood, caressed the mic stand as she sang. The performance made the hairs on my forearms stand to attention.

Our last summer dawn
Our final day is born
It's time to let you go
Oh how my heart is low

The time is growing near
Parting's so hard my dear
But maybe we'll meet again
Good things can't come to an end

Don't cry
The new morning needs a smile
Oh don't you leave behind
Your last glass of summer wine

You're more
Than I've ever wished for
So let your lips meet mine
Our last taste of summer wine

Oh, what a holiday
Just meeting you this way
Fools say it enough
It takes time to fall in love

But we've proved them wrong
Somehow, we must go on
And maybe we'll meet again
Good things can't come to an end.
You're more
Than I've ever wished for
So let your lips meet mine
Our last taste of summer wine

Don't cry, don't cry
The new morning needs a smile
Oh don't you leave behind
Your last glass of summer wine

Summer wine
I can taste it on your lips
Summer wine

The emotional intensity of the performance was palpable, and the band members themselves were visibly moved. It had been an exceptional take, and Ricky didn't hesitate to commend them.

"What a great song," I whispered to Devon.

"Yeah, Kendy's got the magic touch with her compositions. This will be a hit," he replied.

"It's a long way from the punk version of the Fringe," I observed.

"Again, it's Kendy. She brings out the best in them."

As we spoke, the door swung open and the band entered the control room. Greetings and hugs were exchanged. "Hey, that was exceptional, guys. Kendy, who did you meet and lose on the holiday in the lyrics?" I asked.

I realised then why the band was so emotional. "It's how I met Dwip," Kendy disclosed, her voice tinged with sadness. "I was on a holiday my mum had paid for to help me get over a breakup ... I was pregnant ... I met Dwip and she won my heart. We split because she only had a weekend at the resort, and we met up again six months later at the same Uni. The rest is history," she said, her eyes brimming with tears over Dwip's tragic death.

I swiftly changed the topic, pointing towards the studio. Kendy and I moved into the studio amidst the instruments for more privacy.

"I found out that Mrs Charlotte Austin or Charlotte Cross, her maiden name, isn't Charlotte Cross at all but Sarina Abbas."

It hit me like a ton of bricks. "Oh no."

"Yep, that's right. She's like the sister of Tarak Abbas, aka Conway Stevens and Rhett Avalon."

"Now the brother has a blackmail motive," I noted.

"But Charlotte would know that, surely?"

"Yes, you're right ... something's off with this picture. Look, I've got to go and meet Wayne Brown, VP of Valiant. Will you be in tomorrow?"

"Yep, bright and early."

"Okay, see you then. Mighty song, kiddo … and good work on Charlotte, or should I say Sarina."

"Thanks, boss, but I couldn't have done it without Bulldog's help. Charlotte had a clean record, but I pressed Bulldog to dig deeper. He reached out to Interpol, and she surfaced in an inquest a few years ago, linked to her brother's nefarious activities."

CHAPTER
EIGHT

Zhong, accompanied by Detective Lao, was driving through Aberdeen, passing Jumbo Kingdom with its flotilla of junks and boats. Notable for the Jumbo and Tai Pak floating restaurants, the Jumbo had mysteriously sunk in 2022 while being towed from Hong Kong to Cambodia. The Tai Pak, closed for a decade, was set to reopen soon.

Zhong and Lao were responding to a call about a body found under the Ap Lei Chau Bridge, near the Aberdeen Tennis and Squash Centre.

Lao parked in the sports facility's car park, where a security guard met them. He led them through the complex, past a tennis court and along a narrow pathway through trees to the water's edge under the bridge's flyover. En route, the guard explained that a club member crossing the Ap Lei Chau Bridge in the pedestrian lane, had spotted the body and alerted him. Upon investigation, he found the remains. Approaching a small backwater creek, the guard shone a torch on the bank, revealing a dismembered body, causing Lao to vomit. Despite the effluent's stench, Zhong, with a handkerchief over his nose, knelt by the remains, still clothed, and retrieved a business card from the top pocket of the corpse's jacket.

Back at the hotel suite, Charlie, seated in the lounge area, answered his cellphone. It was Zhong. Glancing at Nick, who was engrossed in the 'South China Morning Post', Charlie's expression turned sombre.

He placed the phone on the coffee table.

"That was Zhong at a crime scene in Aberdeen. They found the dismembered body of Brutus Solomona," he informed Nick gravely.

Nick lowered the newspaper, massaging the bridge of his nose, his eyes squinting. "There goes our lead."

He locked eyes with Charlie. "You realise it's now serious and can only get worse. You're stuck in the middle of a triad war over the ownership of Utopia 8. From my experience, they'll stop at nothing to get what they want. This is far worse than what Axis and I experienced with the triads Charlie—this could involve the top four most powerful triad organisations in the world vying for your sixty percent. We need to talk to Axis right now."

I received a call from Charlie just as I was stepping out of the elevator on the 30th floor of the Valiant building.

"Hey Charlie, can't talk long; I'm about to go into a meeting. What's up?"

"Nick and I agree we need you here; things are heating up."

"Okay, leave it with me. I'll work out what I can do; I'm up to my ears in a case."

"I understand. I'll just put Nick on."

"Hey Axis, remember dealing with the Sun Yee On here?" Nick said.

"Sure do."

"Well, this is ten times worse. We need you, kemosabe."

"I hear you, Tonto."

Knowing Nick's urgency meant the situation was critical, but I needed to wrap up my current case before heading to Hong Kong.

I entered Vice President Brown's office reception area and was greeted by a bespectacled blonde receptionist. Her flirtatious glance was unmistakable as she asked me to take a seat. After a brief wait, a door opened and Wayne Brown beckoned me into his office.

It was a grander affair than Dicky's. We shook hands, and he invited me to sit in the lounge area.

"Take a JD?" he offered, revealing his discerning taste.

"Do fish swim?" I replied. "Neat, thanks."

He prepared two neat drinks, brought them over with the bottle, and sat opposite me.

"Never been one for diluting the nectar of the gods with anything," he remarked.

"I'll second that," I agreed, raising my glass in a toast.

"How can I be of help?" he asked, his demeanour friendly.

I described Mrs Austin's commission to find and stop the person sending her threats.

"Yes, so I hear. A terrible thing," he sympathised.

"To do that, I need to unravel what happened on the Raincoat the night Royce was lost."

"Okay."

"Can you please set the scene for me?"

"Sure. I was with Captain Edwards, Charlotte was next to the mainmast arguing with Avalon, about what, I know not. At the stern, Joe, Camille, and Royce were arguing ... so you could say we were the meat in the sandwich."

"Do you know what that argument was about?"

"Yes, actually. The two grandchildren wanted a seat on the board. It was common knowledge, and they were thinking with Royce marrying Charlotte, which came as a surprise to everyone, their chance was now more remote."

"And how was that received by Royce?"

"Not well. He wasn't one for being dictated to ... anyhow, she must've flown off at the mouth, which she's more than capable of, and the old man gave her a clip over the ear. She ran off to give Charlotte an earful, and I went to see if Royce was okay."

"Was he okay?"

"No, he was pretty shaken."

"Where was Joe?"

"He'd taken off after his sister."

"Then what happened?"

"Royce, in his inimitable fashion, turned on me. I wasn't in the mood for family tumult, so I started back to the helm. But something stopped me, a noise I think, and I turned around and Royce had gone. I looked over the stern, called out for Joe when I saw the old boy's captain hat bobbing in the wake."

"Okay, so can you explain how a man with such experienced sealegs could go overboard?"

"No."

He refilled our glasses with two fingers each.

"Could you hazard a guess?" I asked.

"Yes, fuming, he yelled at me, and when I turned my back, ignoring him, he was so angry, he went to lean on the stern rail, missed it, and went over."

I finished my JD and gave him a pointed look. "Mr Brown, you stand to gain from Royce's death..."

"Yes, you won't get an argument out of me on that. Everyone else stands to gain as well. Look, if you're looking for murder, you've missed the boat. It was definitely an accident."

"Will Mrs Austin agree to go public?"

"She already has. Plus, the insurance came through, and she officially owns forty percent of Valiant, eleven percent is to be split between the grandchildren."

"So, she's still the major shareholder..."

"Yes, and chairperson."

"Are you alright with that?"

"Yes, it will ultimately be better than it was."

"With the float?"

"Yes, indeed."

"So who is the biggest loser, in your opinion?"

"Lincoln Austin. He got nothing."

"Was he ever in the company?"

"Yes, he was CEO, but the old boy sacked him and gave it to his younger son Dallas."

"Why did he sack him?"

"He claimed he had an affair with wife number six."

"Did he?"

"I think it might have been the other way around. Let's just say wife number six enjoyed the company of men."

"Did she get anything from the divorce?"

"Only Lincoln as a husband."

"I see. So if Charlotte hadn't married Royce…"

"Yes, Lincoln would be better off because the division of his assets would have favoured the grandchildren more, and his kids would have looked after him."

"Joe and Camille?"

"Precisely."

I stood and extended my hand for a shake, having gathered what I needed. "Thank you for your time, Mr Brown."

"No problem," he said with a congenial smile.

~ ~ ~

A ringing phone jolted Charlie awake. Groping in the dark, he answered groggily, "Hello?" The call instantly energized him. He dressed hastily and headed out to find Nick, who was still up, lounging and watching a film. Nick sat up, instantly aware something was amiss.

"We need to go to Utopia," Charlie announced with a sense of urgency.

Nick glanced at his watch; it was 1 AM. "What's happened?"

"Laila rang me, it's her and Ryan's last night at the club. There are three guys there asking for me, hassling Ryan."

As Nick put on his shoes, he asked, "Too late to call Zhong, are they triads?"

"She thinks so."

"Okay, unarmed, there's not much we can do."

"I know, but our presence might prevent them from giving Ryan a beating."

Nick quickly used the house phone to order a car and chauffeur from the concierge.

The chauffeur dropped them off in D'Aguilar Street, then parked to wait. From there, it was a short walk to Lan Kwai Fong.

Approaching Utopia 8, they encountered a horrifying scene. A crowd had gathered around someone lying on the pavement. Pushing through, Charlie discovered Laila kneeling beside Ryan, whose face was barely recognisable. His eyes were swollen shut, his nose broken and bleeding, lips cut, and his head lay in a spreading pool of blood. Laila looked up at Charlie with tearful eyes, slowly shaking her head. Ryan was dead.

The police arrived and cleared everyone away. Charlie and Nick quickly ushered Laila inside the club, where the music thumped and dancers gyrated. Laila led them through the crowd to the office at the rear. Once inside, they shut out the noise.

"Quickly, before the police come for you, what happened?" Charlie urged.

"Three men came asking for you. When Ryan told them you weren't here, one of them hit him. They dragged him outside and beat him terribly ... one of them kicked him in the face while he was down, and his head hit the wall hard ... I think that's what..." She broke down. "Then they just left him there and walked off as if nothing had happened."

"Do you have any idea who they were?"

"Only when Ryan accused them of being triads, that's what got him kicked in the face."

There was a forceful knock at the door.

"This will be the police. Just tell them what you told me, okay?" Charlie instructed.

She nodded, her expression panicked.

Charlie opened the door to Detective Peng.

"Mr Chan, why am I not surprised to find you here?" he said facetiously.

~ ~ ~

"Come on, Rai, don't be a wimp. It won't hurt; it'll be our own trademark," Wing insisted as the old Foo Man Chu lookalike tattooist finished a skull and crossbones on Wing's wrist. "Check it out, it's way cool."

Rai, with visible hesitation, took Wing's place. Wing firmly grasped Rai's arm to steady him. The old tattoo artist, with his tools at the ready, dipped the needle on the end of the dowel into the black ink, positioned it, then raised his hammer and struck. "Argh!" Rai yelped in pain, as a stream of blood spurted from his wrist, splattering over Wing's face, who responded with a macabre laugh.

Charlie sat up sharply in bed, soaked in sweat, breathing heavily, his heart racing to a disco beat, haunted by Wing's sinister laughter. He turned on the bedside lamp, and scrutinised the six-centimetre tattoo on his right wrist. It wasn't just any skull and crossbones; this skull had a distinctive devilish grin and one missing front tooth.

The clock read 5.45 AM. He lay back down and switched off the lamp. However, sleep remained elusive. Each time he closed his eyes, his mind replayed the scene at the tattooist's, the image of Wing's blood-streaked face haunting him. Silently, he wondered if it was a metaphor for Wing's grisly murder.

~ ~ ~

I returned to the office, the chorus of 'Last Taste' echoing in my mind, along with a whirlpool of questions. Patricia could tell from my expression that I was trying to process everything.

She handed me a JD. "Sit down and talk to me. Keep all that in your head and it'll explode."

I settled on the sofa while she wheeled her chair out from behind her desk to sit and listen.

"First off, what Kendy discovered with Bulldog's help is quite disturbing. It turns out Charlotte, whose real name is Sarina Abbas is…"

"Oh my God, Rhett Avalon's sister!"

"That throws a cat amongst the pigeons. She's either colluding with him or he's blackmailing her," I mused. "Then, I got the most candid insight yet from anyone in the family or company, courtesy of Wayne Brown. He may come across as an old drunk, but in reality, he's a cunning old fox. Joe Austin had said without Brown, Valiant would be non-existent; he's the marketing genius behind it. Despite his age, he's as sharp as ever. Royce's death was definitely an accident, but it was spurred by an argument with Camille and Joe Austin, both jostling for a seat on the Valiant board, with Royce firmly resisting. When he reiterated that there would be no public offering, which would have significantly increased the value of their shares, and then announced that Charlotte would be on the board, Camille blew up and stormed off to have a go at Charlotte."

"So Wayne Brown witnessed all this?"

"Yes, plus he confronted Royce, who was fuming after Joe had gone after Camille. Royce turned on him."

"Sounds like Royce was an aggressive kind of person," Patricia commented.

"Well, I think he was the kind of fellow that didn't take a backward step from anyone. Anyway, he resented Brown's intervention, gave him a piece of his mind, and sent him packing. Brown reckoned Royce probably went to lean on the rail, emotionally upset, missed it and went over. Brown turned around after hearing a noise, and Royce was gone."

"Makes sense."

"So, Royce's death meant the public offer for Valiant that he had so vehemently resisted could happen. Apparently, Charlotte agreed to it with Brown. That appeases everyone except Royce's other son, Lincoln. He's an interesting story; Royce had excommunicated him, accusing him of having slept with his sixth wife, who liked to play around. Once divorced, she married Lincoln."

"How long ago was that?"

"Around 2000, I think," I replied. "Why?"

"So that makes Joe and Camille the offspring of that marriage."

"You know, I never thought of that. How intriguing ... that

certainly explains some things."

"What?"

"Well, I'd say the poison pen letter came from one of the Lincoln Austin family members. Maybe I should talk to the wife?"

"That'd be difficult. Remember the curse of one accidental death every three years? Well, three years ago, she fell down a staircase in her home and broke her neck."

"Well, that limits it to three..."

"What about Mr alias Rhett, Conway, Tarak?"

"He's easy to check out, just need to ask his sister whether he should be a suspect. Can you get her on the line? Oh, and then I need to fly out to Hong Kong."

CHAPTER NINE

I was sitting in my office, lost in thought, when Patricia entered and snapped me out of my reverie.

"Got hold of Charlotte. She doesn't want to talk over the phone. Wants to meet ASAP at her apartment. It's in the same building as Camille's, even on the same floor."

"Damn, I was hoping to wrap it up and fly out."

"By the sound of her voice, I'd say that might be on hold."

"Okay, what's the last flight out of JFK to Hong Kong tonight?"

"Cathay Pacific has a direct flight from Terminal 8 at midnight, lands 6 am tomorrow Hong Kong time."

"Book it business class, I'm a Oneworld Frequent Flyer. Here's the card. Ask them for an upgrade, you never know your luck in the big city."

Twenty minutes later, I found myself in Charlotte's lavish apartment. Compared to Camille's, which was worth twelve million, this one was easily double that. The interior, however, was desperately in need of a make-over. The manservant directed me to the living room, indicating where to sit. I defied his instruction, choosing instead to stand by the window. Only after he left, did I take the opposite chair, just for the fun of it.

Charlotte entered, dressed in flowing chiffon, and paused for me to stand, which I did.

"Mrs Austin."

"Please sit, would you like a drink?"

A butler, resembling Jeeves in a monkey suit, awaited my request.

"I'll take a JD on the rocks, thank you."

She gestured, and he went off to fetch the drink.

"You've questioned most of the immediate family and staff. Have you come to any conclusions?"

"Yes, but first, a few queries for you."

"Go ahead," she replied with a hint of smugness.

"Is there any reason not to eliminate your brother from suspicion?"

"You could have asked me earlier to save time, but yes, you can eliminate him."

"Are you aware he's a wanted man?"

"Yes, but I don't believe that's relevant to this case."

"Oh, I think it is."

"How so?"

"If we can uncover his identity and criminal record, so could someone looking to discredit you."

"And you think that's happened?"

"There's a big chance, yes. Why didn't Royce have you sign a prenup like his other wives?"

"You'd have to ask him."

I let that go. "When did you agree with Wayne Brown to go public?"

Her answer was hesitant. "Two days before Royce's death."

"So, whoever sent the threat didn't know about the public offering. Could they have known you were going to marry Royce?"

"Only Royce, the captain, and perhaps Brown and Wilks knew," she said firmly.

"They claim Royce hadn't told them. What about your brother?"

"Yes, he knew."

"Did Royce know he's your brother?"

She looked uneasy. "Yes, otherwise he wouldn't have let him near me."

"Are you being blackmailed, Mrs Austin?"

She abruptly left the room, returning moments later with an envelope, which she handed to me. Inside was a sympathy card predicting her death in seven days.

"It was hand-delivered here this morning. So I think you need to quickly determine who it is and stop them, or I might not last a week."

"You didn't answer my question. Are you being blackmailed?"

"Yes."

"Why didn't you tell me?"

"I was told not to."

"It makes a big difference in the investigation."

"Why, a threat is a threat, isn't it?"

"No. A blackmailer doesn't want you dead; they want something from you. What is the demand?"

"Ten million in crypto."

"By when?"

"The death day."

"How do you know?"

She showed me a text message: "10 mil in crypto within 7 days or I go public."

"Public with what?"

"My background. It would ruin the public offer."

"So, it can only be one person. Your brother … What were you arguing about with him on the yacht that night?"

"He wanted money."

"For silence."

"Yes."

"So you know it's him."

"I only got the demand today; I thought it was just a family crank. How do I deal with it?"

"Blackmail is a class C felony in New York. This is a case for the cops."

"No, I couldn't live with myself if I had my brother arrested."

"Can you speak with him, negotiate?"

"He's impossible to negotiate with," she said worriedly.

"He won't harm you. If you're unwilling to involve the law, the only option is to negotiate his silence. You didn't tell Royce he was your brother, did you?"

"No."

"Okay, no more lies. Do exactly as I say. Tell no-one, and don't give me any lip. Clear?"

"Yes." She looked down like a naughty girl that had been reprimanded for exposing herself to the little boy next door.

"He might be dangerous, but he's unlikely to harm you. Give me his contacts, and leave it with me. I'll be leaving town for a couple of days, but I'll start the ball rolling with him."

"What, you can't leave now!" she exclaimed.

"My staff are here, I'll only be a phone call away. I just told you, we're playing this my way."

~ ~ ~

Kendy was conversing with Patricia when I entered the office.

"I understand you're jet-setting off to Hong Kong, Mr Stone, leaving us with the poison-pen case?" Kendy inquired with a hint of mischief.

"We're not quite there yet, but at least I've uncovered the identity of the perp, the brother, Mr Avalon alias blah, blah."

I discreetly pressed the keys on my phone to forward a text to Patricia. Her ringtone played, 'Walrus Dreams'.

"What's that tune?" Kendy queried.

"Another Axis composition," Patricia responded, reading the text. "Shall I contact him now?"

"Yes please," I answered, heading to my office.

"Any idea how long you'll be in Hong Kong?" Kendy asked, following me. I settled behind my desk.

"Hopefully just a few days. Nick and Charlie are already there."

"Oh, so Nick's there too? ... I hope you won't miss our big showcase gig at Carnegie Hall next week."

"Have our names on the door, kiddo, I'll be gunning to be there." The desk phone rang; Kendy left as I answered. Patricia's voice informed me she was connecting the call. "Hello, Mr Avalon."

"You're the detective Mrs Austin hired; what do you want from me?"

"I think you know, Mr Avalon, or should I say Stevens or Abbas? Look, I'm across Mrs Austin being your sister, so let's get real—you're trying to blackmail her, sending threatening letters."

There was a momentary silence. I crossed my fingers, hoping he wouldn't disconnect. It was a relief when he finally spoke.

"I might have asked her for some financial help, as family does, but I haven't threatened her," he stated, his voice raspy and accent neutral. His choice of words was somewhat colloquial but no less cunning.

"I'll cut to the chase, Mr Avalon. I can alert Interpol immediately after this call, and they'll be all over you like a cheap suit. So, I have a proposition, are you up for that?"

He sighed, aware I had him over a barrel. "What's the offer?"

"She'll employ you as her bodyguard with a generous salary. You'll receive complimentary accommodation and a comfortable lifestyle, and in return, I won't expose you."

"What sort of salary?"

"You can discuss that with her. She's about to inherit a substantial fortune, so expect it to be sizeable. From my perspective, having interviewed the family, she needs her brother's support. Do we have an agreement, Mr Avalon?"

"You're not leaving me much choice, Mr Stone."

"You might have planned your extortion scheme more effectively, Mr Avalon. Did you genuinely believe you could succeed, given your background?"

"No, but understand, my sister is exceedingly frugal. It required leverage to extract any financial support. I came here to escape that history, Mr Stone."

"Well, don't jeopardise your fresh start with a poorly executed extortion racket, Mr Avalon."

"I understand. Thank you. And about the threats? They definitely weren't from me, but how can I assist you in stopping them?"

"I'm departing for overseas tonight. Monitor the concierge at her apartments and keep an eye on the mail for any further threats. She's been warned she has only seven days. Stay close to her. She has my number; contact me if there's trouble. You have martial arts training, correct?"

"Yes."

"Then use it to protect her. She's not only your sister but also your benefactor. Understand? I'll inform her of our agreement, and you'll meet her soon. Occupy a room in her apartment and act as her bodyguard."

"Thanks, Mr Stone."

I ended the call and immediately contacted Charlotte. "Mrs Austin, I've just spoken with him. You now have a bodyguard. Compensate him well, offer him the spare room, and it's a mutually beneficial arrangement. No, he wasn't behind the threats, so your adversary remains at large. That's why I've arranged for Rhett to be hired. Be generous with his payment. He's well aware that any misconduct will lead me to notify the authorities. No worries, keep him close. Reach out if needed."

I hung up, content with the arrangement but still puzzled over the identity of the poison-pen author. My suspicion lingered on either Lincoln Austin or one of his offspring.

Patricia entered. "How did it go?"

"Successfully. He's now her personal bodyguard, kills two birds with one stone...."

She perched on the edge of my desk, smiling. "Ha! You being the stone..."

"Yep, the extortion ends, and she gains protection from the poison-pen author."

"So Avalon wasn't the culprit?"

"Apparently not. It seemed coincidental that the letters and the blackmail demands both mentioned a seven-day deadline."

"Do you trust him?"

"Yes, he's aware of the leverage I hold. It's a powerful deterrent."

She leaned in and kissed me. "I'm going to miss you, Axis Stone."

~ ~ ~

I scored a win with Cathay Pacific; they upgraded me to first class. After indulging in a couple of glasses of bubbly, a gastronomic triumph for dinner, and three or four JDs, I was sufficiently mellowed to hit the hay and slept soundly all the way to Hong Kong.

~ ~ ~

I entered the Mandarin Oriental lobby at 7:40 am and was promptly relieved of my bags. There was a message at reception to meet the guys at the Clipper Lounge; Patricia, in her usual efficiency, had obviously informed them of my expected arrival time.

I located them on the mezzanine. Within an hour, I was fully briefed.

"Any idea who attacked Brutus and Ryan?" I asked.

"We're pretty sure it was the same culprit, possibly the murderer of my father as well," Charlie said.

"What does Zhong have to say?"

Nick glanced at his watch. "He'll be here shortly."

"We haven't informed him about Ryan," Charlie mentioned.

"One thing's certain, he'd already know," I added.

"We've appointed Laila as the PA for the new office," Nick shared.

"Cat Street," I chuckled. "Eager to check it out; it's a fantastic address."

Zhong approached us. I stood to greet him. "Zhong, how's it going, mate?"

Zhong greeted me with a warm smile. "Axis, great to see you. These lads will need your expertise; things are getting rather ugly."

He sat down, and a waitress approached. We ordered coffees for everyone.

"Did you hear about Ryan Khan last night?" Charlie asked.

"Yes, I received a report from Detective Peng first thing this morning. You were at the scene."

"We arrived post-mortem, but only just, according to Laila, who witnessed it," Nick said.

"It seems multiple triad clans are vying for your shares in Utopia 8, Charlie, and they're willing to resort to murder," Zhong stated solemnly.

"So, Brutus Solomona was found?" I inquired.

Zhong nodded gravely. "Yes, we had to reconstruct him for identification."

"That severe, huh?" I remarked.

"It's officially an OCTB case now, and Ryan's murder adds to the urgency. Charlie, any word from Wong?"

"I'm expecting a call this morning."

"Any leads on who's behind this, Zhong?" I probed.

"My suspicion is one of the smaller clans. It doesn't fit the modus operandi of the Chiu Group, Sun Yee On, or 14K. I consulted with the new Red Pole of Sun Yee On—remember, Axis, you took out their previous enforcer—about their interest in Utopia 8, and he confirmed their intention to bid. However, I doubt the 14K or the Wo Group's involvement, the latter being your partner already. The likely suspects could be among the big four: Leun Group, Tan Yee, Macau Chai, or the Tung Group, perhaps the Big Circle gang or the Hunan Gang. But my bet is on the Red Dragon, a faction that emerged post-1997 handover, always striving to gain prominence— they're notoriously ruthless."

Charlie's phone rang. He excused himself to take the call. Returning a few minutes later, he announced that Wong had four potential offers for him to consider.

"Can he disclose the bidders, or are they anonymous?" Zhong queried.

"Anonymous," Charlie confirmed, resettling in his seat.

CHAPTER
TEN

Later that day, we convened with the lawyer Michael Wong at the Cat Street offices. I was impressed by the office setup and requested a copy of the logo design for our New York office.

I perceived Wong as a quintessential mercenary lawyer, swayed by the highest bidder, a trait that made him susceptible to corruption. It was considerate of Charlie to involve us in what could have been a private family affair, but to Charlie, we were family.

"Since departing the office, two additional offers have come in," Wong disclosed.

"Is there a deadline, Mr Wong?" I asked.

"Well, yes Mr Stone … according to Mr Tan Fang, president of Circle Three, there is…"

"I'm not averse to a deadline, Mr Wong, but I wish to remind you that I am your client, not Mr Fang," Charlie interjected firmly.

"Yes, my apologies, Mr Chan."

"Alright, please list the offers," Charlie asked.

Wong read from his phone. "Four bids of 8 million, one of 8.5 million, and two recent offers of 8.6 and 8.7 million."

"It appears someone is privy to the bidding prices, otherwise there wouldn't be bids of 8.5, 8.6, and 8.7 million dollars … respectively," Nick observed.

"Is this in Hong Kong dollars, Mr Wong?" Charlie inquired.

"No, US dollars, Mr Chan."

I observed Charlie's astonished expression as he nearly toppled from his chair, unaware of Utopia 8's substantial value.

"Charlie, are you familiar with this bidding process?" Nick queried.

"Not in the slightest."

"May I suggest?" Nick offered.

"By all means," Charlie responded with gratitude.

"We propose creating a questionnaire. The bidder providing the most satisfactory answers to Mr Chan will be chosen. Inform the bidders that Mr Chan desires the asset in the best possible hands."

Wong's complexion turned ashen. "Sir, your current partner, Circle Three, will not be pleased. They've explicitly stated their aversion to a triad partnership."

"Mr Wong, we're unaware of the identities of any bidders, hence that won't influence our decision."

"I'm open to allowing Circle Three to match any selected bid ... would that appease Mr Fang?" Charlie suggested.

Wong, visibly relieved, stuttered, "Y... y...yes, I believe that would be acceptable."

Following Wong's departure, Nick solemnly remarked, "If ever a conflict was to erupt over this, it would be now."

Laila's voice interrupted from outside, "Mr Chan, it's Laila."

Charlie stood. "Please, come in, Laila."

She entered, radiating charm. Charlie introduced her. She was precisely the type of woman my former self would have pursued, and though still appealing, I consciously chose to ignore that primal impulse.

"How are you coping after such a harrowing experience?" Nick inquired, genuinely concerned.

"It's challenging to erase from memory ... I thought being here today would serve as a useful distraction."

Charlie escorted her to reception and phoned Carmen in LA to have her guide Laila in aligning the office with the Sunset office's operations.

"So, what's next?" Nick asked.

"Whoever eliminated Brutus and Ryan might attempt a kidnapping to coerce Charlie for bidding favour. He should warn Carmen." I stood, approached Charlie in reception, and advised, "Mate, it's probable one of the bidders will attempt a kidnapping to pressure you. Inform Carmen, and suggest Enzo keeps a watchful eye."

Charlie acknowledged, took the phone from Laila, and conveyed the message to Carmen. Returning to Nick, he added, "We should also be vigilant regarding Laila; she lives alone."

I agreed.

By early afternoon, fatigue had set in. We opted to return to the Mandarin for some relaxation and strategic planning. Laila joined us, having gathered a few essentials from her apartment for her stay. She settled into the spare room, engrossed in her phone, while we occupied the lounge area.

Charlie received a call from Wong, confirming that Fang had agreed to the negotiation terms. After the call, he remarked, "We need Zhong's expertise on the best approach to handle this."

"First, we should compose the questionnaire," Nick suggested, ever-focused on business protocols.

It took us about an hour to formulate the twelve questions. Once finalised, Charlie relayed them to Wong.

Nick was confident that one of his questions would reveal whether a bidder was triad-affiliated or not. Charlie's plan was to offer the deal to a non-triad bidder, should one emerge. The pivotal question sought proof of financial viability—essentially, evidence of the ability to pay. Once we received verifiable proof, Zhong would scrutinise the details with the tax department. Any triad-sourced black money would be exposed.

Nick led us to Ando, a restaurant not far from the Mandarin, known for its unique blend of Japanese and Argentine cuisine and one of his favourites. During our meal, Charlie was informed by Wong that he had successfully distributed the questionnaire to all contenders. Now, we were in a waiting game.

After indulging in several bottles of sake, we somewhat unsteadily made our way back to the Mandarin for some well-deserved rest.

The following morning, post-breakfast in our rooms, Charlie got an update from Wong. Two of the bidders had withdrawn, likely deterred by the stiff competition or the questionnaire's probing nature.

Our next move was to head to Cat Street. Laila had tasks assigned by Carmen, and we needed to adjust our strategy in light of losing two bidders. Wong informed us that the withdrawn bids were the highest at 8.7 million and another at 8 million. This left the top bid at 8.6 million.

Zhong contacted Nick with a crucial update: CCTV footage from Lan Kwai Fong, utilising facial recognition, identified one of Ryan Khan's attackers as Wan Foon, a prominent enforcer or 'red pole' of the Red Dragon. This confirmed his suspicion that a lesser-known triad clan was involved. Zhong had the resources to confront them with the evidence.

"They'll hand him over, then use legal loopholes to secure his release. Frustrating, but reminiscent of our encounter with Dragon Head Lee Kok Lung of Sun Yee On," Nick recounted.

Charlie received a distressing call from Carmen. It was 11 am in Hong Kong, and 7 pm the previous day in LA. She was shaken. Returning to the office from an appointment, she found two men intimidating the receptionist, Carol. Her sharp retort in Chinese drove them away. Unfortunately, Enzo, returning from a smoke break, clashed with them on the stairs. One assailant stabbed Enzo with a switchblade. Carmen, unable to wait for an ambulance, rushed him to a doctor, who managed to treat the wound, thankfully missing any vital organs.

Relieved, Charlie shared the news with us. It was evident that the Red Dragon's reach extended to LA.

"Seems the Red Dragon are still in the bidding. Maybe we should press Wong to disclose their bid, so we can disregard it," Charlie suggested, angered by the attack on Enzo and the harassment at the office.

"Let Zhong handle it. He's familiar with them and can bypass Wong if necessary," I said.

Nick promptly briefed Zhong on the incident. Surprisingly, Zhong revealed his connection to Zhong Heng Lawyers—Zhong Heng was actually his uncle. When Nick relayed this to us, we were astonished. "I wish he'd shared that sooner; it could've simplified matters."

"In Chinese culture, asking for favours is often avoided; they prefer other means, like bribes," Charlie noted.

"Same in the Philippines," Nick added.

An hour later, Nick received a call from Zhong. The Red Dragon had made the highest offer of 8.6 million.

"Each call is costing me a fortune," Charlie joked.

"Look at the bright side, you'll still be leaving with a shit-load of bread," I reminded him.

Charlie, now smiling broadly, acknowledged, "True."

A while later, Laila entered our office, informing Charlie that she had received a call from Tan Fang's PA at Circle Three. Apparently, Mr Fang was irate about the club being closed the previous night. "She insisted that I should have been managing the club during the hunt for Ryan's replacement," Laila conveyed.

Charlie, displeased with their tone, instructed Laila to get Fang on the line. As she stepped out to make the call, we deliberated on the situation.

"Calm down, Charlie," I advised. "These guys are fixated on profit. Naturally, they'd expect Laila to be there. They're unaware of her involvement with us."

Nick proposed, "This at least confirms Circle Three wasn't behind Ryan's elimination. Otherwise, they would have had a replacement ready."

"True on all counts," Charlie concurred, "But their aggressive, money-driven approach irks me."

"The sooner you're disentangled from this, the better. Associating with these types isn't our style," I said.

"I'd exit immediately if resolving Ki's murder didn't complicate my inheritance," Charlie lamented.

"Here's an idea—use that to your advantage with Fung. Make it clear that solving your father's murder is your priority before any asset liquidation," Nick suggested.

"Actually, I did mention that to him," Charlie said.

"Then let's formalise it. We can have Zhong communicate with his uncle at Zhong Heng Law, who will then inform Michael Wong, that the inheritance will remain frozen until the murder is resolved," Nick elaborated.

"Plus, if it's endorsed by the OCTB, it's unquestionable," I added.

It was a sound strategy. Enlisting one of Hong Kong's largest triad clans could expedite the investigation, especially given their vested interest in a resolution and the likelihood that the culprit was an adversary.

Charlie's conversation with Fong was more measured than anticipated. Instead of reacting with anger, Charlie calmly explained that Laila was in shock and that he had accepted her resignation from Utopia 8. Fong seemed content with this explanation and even inquired about Charlie's progress in solving Ki's murder. Charlie expressed his desire to resolve the matter so he could liquidate the assets and return to LA. The seed was planted.

Fong then mentioned he would assign one of his own staff to temporarily manage the club. He also brought up the issue of profit distribution, revealing he had been holding onto a considerable sum: Ki's share of the club's revenue since his death. Charlie realised that this money, which Ki used to fund Charlie's extravagant education, had now accumulated significantly. Curious, Charlie inquired about the amount, but Fung was reluctant to discuss specifics over the phone, hinting at his desire to keep the matter away from legal scrutiny. It was clear to Charlie that this was unreported income—essentially, black money.

After updating us, Nick suggested, "Looks like we're heading to Macau next."

"I'd prefer to return to LA," Charlie said.

"With black money? The IRS would be all over it. Axis, remember the Fortune Garden in Sydney? One of their partners owns a Macau casino, noted for laundering," Nick explained.

"If you think I'm taking cash to Macau to gamble, you're mistaken," Charlie retorted.

Nick clarified the plan—converting the cash to cryptocurrency for Charlie to manage as he saw fit. Once understanding the logistics of laundering the money into untraceable crypto, Charlie was noticeably more at ease.

Zhong was on board with the plan and reached out to his uncle, setting off a chain of events. Calls from Wong and Fung followed. Wong expressed displeasure about the intrusion of the OCTB, and we enjoyed Charlie giving him a piece of his mind about just doing his job. Then came a call from Fang, surprisingly pleasant. He invited Charlie to a lunch meeting with two of his executives at one of his restaurants in Tsim Sha Tsui. Charlie accepted, stating he would bring his partners.

Nick noted Fang's mention of 'one' of his restaurants, wondering how many he owned.

We dropped Laila at the Mandarin and took the Star Ferry across the harbour to Tsim Sha Tsui. The journey was less than ideal, with windy and rainy weather making the harbour choppy. My dislike for maritime travel resurfaced, but thankfully we docked before I got sick.

We navigated through a maze of subterranean shops, emerging on Nathan Road, close to our destination: the Circle Three Restaurant.

Running five minutes late due to the weather, we entered the Chinese cuisine establishment and were led to a private room at the back. The setting reminded me of a previous encounter with triads in a gambling room behind the Four Fingers Club in Kowloon.

CHAPTER
ELEVEN

Inside The Circle Three Restaurant, we found Tan Fang seated with his red pole enforcer, Da ye Zhu, and his white fan, Ge Ge. They exuded a gangster aura. Fang introduced them and Charlie introduced us.

Nick later explained that Da ye Zhu meant 'big wild boar' and Ge Ge 'brother'.

A lavish feast ensued, and Fang proved to be a much more hospitable host than Lee Kok Lung, the Dragon head of Sun Yee On had been. Post-feast, while enjoying fine brandy, Da ye Zhu acknowledged me as a local hero.

Puzzled, I asked, "How so? I don't understand."

"Because you took out Sun Yee On's red pole enforcer, Fatty Tung, and white paper fan, Soy Ling Chu," he replied gruffly.

Fung elaborated, "Mr Stone, your efforts to save Mr Sun Ty's restaurant in Sydney, The Golden Dragon, and his family, did not go unnoticed." He then toasted to both Nick and me for our roles in resolving the crisis.

During the conversation, Charlie learned that around two million US dollars, his share from the club, was waiting for him in cash. Fang proposed a way to launder the money with only a one percent fee, a far better deal than losing forty percent to the IRS.

Fang then suggested that if Charlie sold his sixty percent shareholding, he could invest in shares of the club, earning a sizable monthly dividend with a guarantee, thus avoiding taxes on the sale.

Nick mentioned our Hong Kong division of Stone, Vargas and Chan Investigations, and Ge Ge inquired about our objectives. Charlie confirmed our first case was to solve Ki Chan's murder. Ge Ge revealed suspicions about the Red Dragon's involvement in the three murders.

Da ye Zhu suggested a typically triad method: capturing one of their men to extract a confession. Fang revealed a plan to capture their red pole at the Four Fingers Restaurant during a high-stakes card game that night.

We left the restaurant feeling confident about our new alliance with Fang.

The return trip to Central was less distressing. The swell had eased, and Nick kept me engaged in conversation on the ferry, which helped me avoid feeling nauseous. Our short walk from the Star Ferry pier to the Mandarin was sheltered from the drizzle. As we entered the lobby, a well-dressed man in a business suit bumped into Charlie, causing him to drop his folder. The man, apologetic, bent down to pick it up, revealing a tattoo on his wrist. Both Charlie and I noticed it, and I could see Charlie's face turn pale. The man handed the folder back and quickly vanished into the crowd.

In the elevator, Charlie's silence and distant look didn't escape my notice.

Once in our room, I asked, "Mate, are you alright? You look like you've seen a ghost."

"I think I have," he replied, settling into the lounge.

"What's this about?" Nick inquired.

"When that guy bumped into me in the foyer and I dropped the folder, he picked it up, and I noticed he had a tattoo the same as this on his wrist." Charlie pulled back his cuff to show us a skull and crossbones tattoo.

Laila, who had joined us, looked on curiously.

"A skull and crossbones. Must be a few people with that tattoo," Nick remarked. "Why does it bother you?"

"Because this tattoo has a smiling skull with a missing tooth, see?"

We examined it closely, and indeed, it matched his description.

"Only my friend who was murdered when we were teenagers and I have this tattoo. An old tattooist, long since passed, made it our own. Only my friend Wing and I had them. It was our personal coat of arms."

"That's what has you freaked out," I observed. "It's either an uncanny coincidence or your friend didn't die."

"Exactly," Charlie said, his expression troubled.

Later, after a light snack for dinner, with Laila being the only one with an appetite, Wong called Charlie. He offered to drop off three completed questionnaires needing Charlie's signature.

Charlie went down to meet Wong in Chater Road, behind the Mandarin. An hour passed without Charlie's return, so I phoned him, but it went to voicemail. Nick called Wong, who claimed to have not called Charlie and had no questionnaires to deliver. We realised then that Charlie had been abducted.

I immediately phoned Zhong to inform him of the situation. He mobilised his team and said he'd join us in our room within fifteen minutes. The recent incident with Brutus heightened our concern for Charlie's safety. By the time Zhong arrived, Nick and I were pacing like caged animals, desperate to find Charlie.

Zhong brought a sense of calm with his logical approach. As we recounted the events of the past twenty-four hours, Zhong highlighted two critical points: our meeting with Fang and the stranger who had bumped into Charlie in the lobby.

I pressed him to elaborate on why the meeting with Fang could be problematic.

"Because they're about to act on your behalf to kidnap the red pole of the Red Dragon. The Red Dragon wouldn't know that, but they've likely anticipated it. They'd have tailed you to your meeting. Everyone knows the Circle Three Restaurant is Wo Shing Wo territory. The triad gangs keep track to avoid entering rival territory. So, it's reasonable to assume the Red Dragon would do the same.

Ransom is a common negotiation tactic for triads, especially when they hit a wall, which they have ... They knew we'd eventually link them to the murders of Brutus, Ryan, and probably Ki."

"Sour grapes," I commented.

"Exactly. Now, tell me about the tattoo."

I recounted the story as I knew it: Charlie, then known as Rai, was a street kid in Kowloon Tong, running with his friend Wing. They witnessed a triad execution and Wing was captured. Charlie found refuge with Ki Chan and his wife, later being sent to Ki's brother in Los Angeles. Ki Chan later legally adopted Charlie to keep him safe.

"Charlie's friend Wing didn't die," Zhong explained. "He survived and is now the dragon head of the Red Dragon. That's who bumped into Charlie in the lobby ... and it was deliberate. That's who has him now."

"Do you know this for a fact?" Nick asked.

"Yes, the Wing story is part of triad folklore. Charlie would have known if he were more familiar with Hong Kong, but his avoidance kept him unaware."

I flopped back in my chair when the realisation dawned on me. "This was about more than just the club sale ... it's redemption. The Red Dragon probably didn't even want the club; Wing Lee was just trying to flush Charlie out, he probably learned of Ki's role as his adoptive father when they murdered him."

"How did Charlie's mother die?" I wondered aloud.

"That's another angle," Zhong mused. "Maybe that was how Wing learned Charlie had been adopted."

"Okay, one way or the other, it's motive," Nick said. "So, what can we do about it? Do you think Wing wants to kill him?"

"Maybe not, he might want to use Charlie to undermine his rival, Tan Fung."

"We need to do what we did last time," I suggested. "We need to meet the dragon head, Wing Lee."

"Last time was different Axis; we had something they wanted,"

Nick countered.

"I'm not so sure about that. I doubt Wing Lee knows that we're aware of his connection to Charlie. If we keep it under wraps, and Charlie doesn't give it away, we could negotiate his return for a ransom."

Zhong, however, thought differently. "But Lee can already negotiate directly with Charlie since he owns what Lee desires—Utopia 8."

"Then there's only one other way ... we need to ensure Fang and his men capture the Red Dragon's red pole tonight at the Four Fingers. That would give us a bargaining chip."

Considering my local hero status with the Wo Shing Wo, I was chosen to update Fang. I called him.

"Mr Fang, we have a serious problem."

"Can I be of assistance?" he said coolly.

"Yes, I've put you on speaker for my partner Nick to hear. We believe Charlie Chan has been kidnapped by the Red Dragon."

"Do you think they aim to leverage his life against the shareholding?"

"That's our belief."

"How did it happen?"

"A man bumped into Charlie in the lobby of the Mandarin, knocking a folder from Charlie's hands. When the man retrieved it, Charlie noticed a tattoo on his wrist identical to his own. They both received those tattoos as street kids."

"I'm familiar with the story but didn't realise the boy who escaped was Charlie Chan."

Nick and I raised eyebrows; it had obviously become an urban myth.

"He was known as Rai back then. Ki Chan saved him and later adopted him, sending him to live with his brother in LA."

"Ah, it all makes sense now. So, to Wing Lee, this is revenge because Rai left him for dead," Fang said.

"I'm not sure, Charlie mentioned that Wing told him to run."

"Different to the legend but perhaps more accurate, these things change over time. So then it is probably about me. Wing must want the major share in Utopia 8 to gain an upper hand over me. It would strengthen his position within his clan, which has been weakening."

"We need the red pole to barter for Charlie," I claimed.

"You'll need more than the red pole to negotiate for Charlie; you'd need Wing himself."

"How can we accomplish that?"

"He will also be at the Four Fingers tonight. Perhaps my men capturing the red pole will create enough distraction for you to seize Wing Lee? But remember, you will only get one shot at it. If you fail, Chan will surely be killed."

"I'll discuss it with Nick and get back to you."

After explaining the situation to Nick and Zhong, I sensed their apprehension.

"Tricky," Zhong remarked. "Like he said, you only have one chance, and the consequences of failure are dire."

"What's your opinion, Nick?"

"We know the area. We'll need weapons and backup, especially if we use the alley where we had that fight, Axis."

"Yes, it's secluded, with a dead end. If we can corner him there and have your men ready in ambush, we might stand a chance."

After agreeing on the finer details, I called Carmen to update her about Charlie. She initially expected the police to intervene but understood the delicacy of the situation when I explained that any police involvement could lead to Charlie's immediate execution. She realised our plan carried risks, but there was no avoiding the danger to Charlie's life.

I called Fang back to plan the operation at the Four Fingers.

Zhong had arranged for two Glock 19 pistols to be delivered to our hotel. We planned to leave the hotel at eleven, with the card game starting at midnight. Fang had set up Nick to play and for me to accompany him. Nick had to transfer twenty thousand US dollars into a nominated crypto account for Four Fingers, to be used for wagering, with chips drawn against the amount.

Sitting on the lounge, checking the Glock, I felt as though I was preparing for battle. Laila entered and sat opposite me, looking lovely in a Japanese print robe.

"How can you do this?" she asked, watching me.

"Do what?" I replied, pushing in the clip.

"Go into a fight ... Both of you could be killed tonight. Wing Lee saw you in the Mandarin lobby, didn't he?"

"I have to take that risk. Thing of it is we could be killed any night; this one just happens to have a good purpose."

"Doesn't it worry you? You seem so calm."

"That's just the hardened exterior. Inside, I'm freaking out," I said, forcing a wry smile.

"I can't imagine you freaking out, Mr Stone."

"Don't worry, I've had my moments. I just hope tonight isn't one of them. You know, some people like comfort in life; I've always preferred a challenge. Like my friend who freefalls from planes, or another who races cars. They risk their lives without a second thought. It's the same for me. This is my gig. Tonight, we have to save a friend's life. The mob that's kidnapped him is ruthless, as you've seen. The person behind these crimes needs to be brought to justice. We're doing our bit to make the world that little bit safer."

"I'm honoured to work for you, Mr Stone."

I took her hand. "Call me Axis, we dispense with formalities at SVC," I chuckled.

"Are you going to call Patricia?"

"No, it would only worry her."

As if on cue, my cellphone rang with 'The Terrible Tango', Patricia's ID showing.

"Funny you should mention her..." I moved to the window, answering the call. "Hey Trish, just mentioned your name, and here you are."

"I got the vibe," she replied warmly. I imagined her smiling eyes.

"Carmen called. I can't believe Charlie's been kidnapped. You and Nick are going after him, aren't you?"

"Yes, there's no other way. Is Carmen alright?"

"A bit shaken, but she's tough. Look, I know you've got enough on your plate, but you need to know, Charlotte was found dead in her apartment this morning."

"What? By whom?"

"Avalon."

"He was there during her murder?"

"I don't know the details. Bulldog and Kendy are at the crime scene. I'll update you soon."

"Talk tomorrow, my time. We're going in tonight for Charlie."

"Oh, okay." After a pause, she added, "Don't get yourself killed or anything, okay, Axis Stone? Promise me." I could tell by her voice she was tearing up.

"I promise. Got to go now, kiddo. Don't worry about me, this sort of stuff comes with the gig. Talk tomorrow, okay."

"I love you."

"Second that," I replied, wondering why I so struggled to say those three simple words.

CHAPTER
TWELVE

We knew we'd be electronically scanned for weapons upon entering Four Fingers, so we concealed our guns in the dark alleyway outside the entrance. The success of our mission hinged on timing; we needed to swiftly extract Wing Lee from the club once Da ye Zhu and his men created a diversion. We were also relying on remaining unrecognised.

Zhong had cautioned that the dragon head of Sun Yee On, Lee Kok Lung, whom we had previously encountered, was likely to be at the card game. It was a reasonable expectation, given that the Four Fingers was located in Sun Yee On territory.

Upon entering the private club, a bouncer checked us off a list on his phone and then led us through the club, which had only a few patrons, to a red door down a narrow corridor. He opened it, and we entered the gambling den, pausing just inside the door. I scanned the room, noting its four gambling tables—one for mah-jong, two for poker, and another for blackjack. The club had undergone a makeover since our last visit, now exuding an air of class. Ceiling and exhaust fans circulated the air, clearing the smoke from numerous smokers, making it more bearable for non-smokers like Nick and me.

Fifteen patrons sat on barstools along the long bar that extended down the side wall, while around a dozen more were scattered at tables, with four players at the blackjack table. The clientele appeared more up-market than previously, with red carpeting, low lighting, and spotlights over the gaming tables. I was the only Westerner, and the only women present were three waitresses and the croupier at the blackjack table. We were greeted by a well-groomed man in his forties, dressed in a tailored suit.

"Welcome, Mr Vargas," he said in heavily accented English.

"This is my guest, Mr Axis," Nick said.

I nodded in acknowledgement.

"The game will commence in thirty minutes. In the meantime, please enjoy complimentary champagne at the bar," he said, gesturing in that direction.

As other guests entered through the door behind us, I recognised Da ye Zhu among them. We headed to the bar to collect our champagne. The subtle Chinese music playing was slightly louder at the bar. The place was nearing capacity with about thirty people. I looked up, counting six CCTV cameras around the perimeter, with none positioned over the gambling tables for obvious reasons. I also observed four security guards stationed at each corner of the square room, with one at the entrance, all wearing earpieces, suggesting they were connected to each other and likely a control room monitoring the CCTV. By now, facial recognition would have likely profiled me; Nick's identity was already known.

A beautiful young woman in a traditional cheongsam glided in from a rear door, distributing individual digital wallets to the players.

The most crucial task for us now was to identify Wing Lee.

Nick and I were joined at the bar by Da ye Zhu and his associate. We maintained a discreet distance, avoiding direct eye contact. Zhu collected two flutes of champagne and, as he moved past Nick, he muttered something in Chinese. Nick shot me a quick glance, using a subtle Filipino gesture of pursed lips to direct my attention towards a man seated with two others at a nearby table. I casually sipped my drink while keeping an eye on the target. As he reached for his glass, his arm extended enough to reveal a skull and crossbones tattoo on his wrist—it was Wing Lee. I assumed one of the men seated with him was the red pole Zhu planned to ambush.

The emcee, holding a cordless microphone, positioned himself in the room's centre and welcomed everyone in Chinese. He then switched to English.

"There will be two tables in the challenge stud poker event. The stakes are open, with the best five-card rule, and a limit of nine players per table. Non-players are requested to maintain their seats. Players, please choose your preferred table."

Eighteen men, including Nick, who managed to secure a seat beside Wing Lee, occupied the tables. Zhu and his partner, as well as Wing Lee's two companions, chose not to participate. I scanned the players and was relieved not to recognise Lee Kok Lung, the dragon head of Sun Yee On.

While I knew Nick excelled at mah-jong, his poker skills were unknown to me. Poker, a game of bluff, played to Nick's strengths.

After an hour, I noticed Nick accumulating a substantial amount of chips, whereas Wing Lee seemed to be struggling. Feeling my phone vibrate, I headed to the bathroom to check it, having disabled the ringtone earlier. In an empty cubicle, I sat and read the text from Zhong: he was in position. There was no need for a reply; he would wait for my signal.

Another hour passed, and Nick's winnings had increased, while Wing Lee appeared ready to leave. I decided against ordering another JD. Wing seemed on the brink of departing. Catching Zhu's eye, he winked at me. It was time. I exchanged a knowing glance with Nick, who understood the signal as Wing stood up.

Nick cashed out his chips and joined me. "Looks like you did alright," I observed.

"Tripled the investment. They weren't pleased about me leaving the game up so much. It's a competition; you're expected to keep playing until it gets down to the final two."

Wing Lee and his three companions were heading towards the door, closely followed by Zhu and his associate.

"Let's move," I urged Nick.

As we approached the exit, I sent a pre-written 'Go' text to Zhong.

The club was nearly empty. Wing paused at the exit to speak with the doorman, whom Fang had bribed to delay him, allowing Zhu to exit first.

Nick and I feigned an argument near the door to buy time for Wing to leave. The doorman eventually let them pass, and it was our cue to follow. He handed us our concealed guns as we exited—another part of the plan.

Outside, Zhu and his partner immediately confronted Wing's companions. I approached Wing, pressing the gun into his back. "Walk!" I commanded.

Zhu and his mate, armed with knives, needed Nick's assistance to corral the three men into the alleyway behind Wing and I. As we rounded a corner, Zhong and four police officers emerged from the shadows. One of Wing's men tried to escape, but Zhu swiftly incapacitated him with a stab to the thigh. Zhong allowed Zhu to take the red pole, his police arresting the other two, while we escorted Wing to Zhong's car.

The operation had been executed flawlessly. Not a word was spoken, even during the car ride back to Central, with Wing handcuffed and gazing out of the window.

The cold silence from Wing was deafening as we made our way to Cat Street. I tried to get a single word out of him, but to no avail. I then delved into the story of Charlie's life, detailing the heavy burden of guilt he'd carried for leaving Wing for dead. I narrated the tale with all the emotional weight I could muster, the kind of narrative that could bring a tear to anyone's eye or inspire a movie studio executive.

To my utter astonishment, Wing just chuckled at the end of it, as if the entire narrative had been one big joke. That reaction was the last straw for me. Frustration and disbelief collided, and I blew up. His laughter in the face of such a poignant story, one that had defined Charlie's entire existence, was more than I could bear.

"So, you murder his father, two of his innocent employees, try to frighten his girlfriend in LA, and get his friend stabbed in the process.

For what? To be big time? To impress? And now you kidnap him." I confronted him aggressively. "What the hell are you trying to get Charlie to do? At least tell us that much."

His grin was deranged. He remained silent, so Zhong took over, barking at him in Cantonese. The aggression in his voice was palpable, even Nick winced. I half-expected Zhong to resort to physical violence, but he refrained, and still, Wing sat unfazed by any of it.

Finally, Zhong demanded in English, "Tell me the location of Charlie Chan."

Wing spoke for the first time. "If I'm not heard from by 4 am, his throat will be slit."

It was 3:15 am—a tight, nerve-wracking forty-five-minute window.

Nick interjected, "What do you want?"

"His sixty percent," Wing declared.

"How much are you willing to pay?" Nick pressed.

"Nothing. His life for the club."

Zhong threatened imprisonment for murder, but Wing was unfazed, claiming there was no evidence.

"You would've made the same offer to Charlie. What did he say?" Nick demanded.

"He told me to fuck off."

"Tan Fang doesn't want you as a partner," I pointed out.

"That's bad luck for him," Wing shrugged.

Zhong snarled, "It wouldn't work, you know that."

With time running out, Nick offered, "Twenty percent."

"Fifty," Wing countered.

"Twenty-five," Nick countered back.

"Thirty, and I walk," Wing compromised.

"Done," Nick agreed with a terse nod.

Nick handed Wing his phone. "Make the call."

Once the call was made, Zhong escorted Wing out to his car. Carefully, he handcuffed Wing inside the vehicle, ensuring he couldn't escape or cause any further trouble. After securing him, Zhong returned to us.

"Nice work, Nick," Zhong commented as he walked back in. "It wasn't looking good there for a while."

"He's a tough nut," I muttered.

"Charlie's going to be livid I just cost him four million bucks," Nick mused.

"He owes his life to you," Zhong pointed out.

I found a bottle of JD and some new glasses. Pouring drinks, I raised my glass, "To us."

Right on cue, Charlie walked in. He looked rough, but we hugged him and handed him a JD. We toasted his freedom before Zhong brought Wing in, uncuffed.

Wing faced Charlie with a smug look, but Charlie surprised us all by yelling, "Run, Wing, run!" Wing strolled casually out of the office. Charlie had settled the score; it was over.

Charlie took the news of Nick's deal with Wing in stride.

"So, what will you do with the remaining thirty percent, Charlie?" Zhong inquired.

"Keep it. Now that Fang has Wing's red pole, we have the murderer. He killed Ki and the others; I found out while they had me. I always wanted a non-triad shareholder, and now I've got one, it's me."

The next morning, Zhong called Charlie bright and early. Charlie agreed to press charges against Wan Foon, the Red Pole of the Red Dragon. The rest could be left in the hands of Zhong and the OCTB. They would now contact Tan Fun and arrange to take Foon into custody to face charges. He was confident that with three counts of murder, they could make the charges stick.

We were having a coffee when Charlie got his next call, this time from Tan Fang. It was to be expected that Zhong would've made him aware of the deal for Utopia 8. Surprisingly, Fang wasn't displeased by the deal, as had all expected. He was happy to have the majority shareholding, though not thrilled to be in bed with the Red Dragon, but content that Charlie had decided to retain a stake on equal terms with Wing Lee. He felt it was providence that the two legendary childhood friends ended up partners again. Charlie hadn't thought of it that way, but it did make sense. Fang reminded Charlie of the pool of black money being held for him. He handed the phone to Nick, who arranged for it to be transferred into a crypto account.

Charlie's final act that morning was to phone Michael Wong and give him the details of the shareholding. Wong was the least impressed with the outcome, as Charlie figured he must have been on a finder's fee from Fang, which of course was now nothing but two share transfers.

Then there was the matter of the two properties. Charlie directed Wong to transfer the Cat Street property to his company, Stone, Vargas, and Chan Investigations, LLC (West Coast), and to liquidate the apartment in Kowloon Tong. Wong asked what to do with Ki Chan's three bank accounts, which amounted to twenty thousand Hong Kong dollars and change. Charlie told him to donate it to St. Christopher's Home for street kids and to then close the accounts. Finally, Charlie asked if Wong would represent his personal interests in Utopia 8 and the legal work for Stone, Vargas, and Chan Investigations, Hong Kong. Wong happily agreed.

Laila was happy to continue working for us, so Charlie arranged for Wong to draw up a contract of employment for her.

It had all worked out quite well for Charlie; he'd found his father's murderer, he'd been able to rid himself of the guilt over Wing that he'd carried since his childhood, a new office had been set up with the capable Laila manning it, and he had a share in a business that would provide him a good earn, that he didn't need to worry about, and he had several million in crypto in an account and more coming from the sale of the property.

On the other hand, I needed to get back to the Big Apple quick smart to help Bulldog deal with the murder of Charlotte Austin.

Nick had his expenses covered by his win at poker, so he had no complaints.

Zhong turned up at the Mandarin as we were checking out, Charlie picked up the bill. We were shocked when Zhong confided to us he'd put in his notice with the OCTB.

"So are you moving to another division?" I asked.

"No, I'm going to hang up the boots," Zhong replied. "The wife is pregnant, and the stress of having me constantly at war with triad gangs is just too much for her. I'll find myself something new, maybe go back to university for a criminology degree."

The three of us exchanged a knowing glance, and Charlie said, "Would you consider coming in as a partner in the Hong Kong office of Stone, Vargas, and Chan?"

"You'd run the show here as Asia president," Nick said. "I've got the office in Manila manned by my daughter, then Charlie runs west coast US, Axis in New York handles the east coast."

"We've got the Sydney office still with Rick Malone set to run it, you remember him, he introduced us to you in the first place," I explained.

"Of course I do. Let me talk it over with my wife; I'll let you know by tomorrow."

"Laila here would be your PA," Nick said.

Laila gave us all a big smile. We said our goodbyes and then boarded the limo for the airport. The three of us would catch different flights back to our respective parts of the world, but always together as a team.

CHAPTER
THIRTEEN

CX830 departed Chek Lap Kok at 9:30 am. It was an Airbus 351 with no first class, but I had 11D, a great seat in the centre aisle. I was exhausted, having had no sleep the night before. It made it perfect for me to snore most of the sixteen-hour flight to JFK.

I strolled into the office fresh as a daisy. Trish was over the moon to see me safe and sound, as was Kendy, but in a different sense. I spent an hour filling them in and getting an update from them on the murder of Charlotte Austin.

Kendy said Bulldog had determined that Avalon was clear; the murderer had somehow infiltrated security and poisoned Charlotte's morning coffee. Avalon had the perfect alibi, as he was with the head of building security in his office in the lobby at the time of the murder, going over the daily schedule.

She had been poisoned with Ethylene glycol, antifreeze. At least 100 millilitres had been used; it's odourless, colourless, and sweet tasting. The drug took effect while she was taking her morning swim in the pool, and she subsequently drowned.

"Ironically, she'll be cremated exactly as the first invitation she'd received had indicated," Kendy concluded.

"Yes, well, Avalon would be eliminated right away because he needed her to stay alive. The only beneficiaries to her dying would be those with shares in Valiant, because her shares were not transferable; no-one could inherit them," I explained.

"I don't get it," Kendy said.

"She could only sell the shares if she had a supporting majority vote from the board, and the shares could not be passed to an heir," I clarified.

"So, only the board stands to gain," Patricia stated.

"Perhaps," I said, unsure, "and, I suppose family members not on the board might also benefit. Wayne Brown can answer that for us, Trish, can you get him on the phone, please?"

While Trish called, Kendy said, "I'm glad you made it back in time for tonight's Carnegie Hall gig."

"Wouldn't miss it for the world," I lied; I'd forgotten all about it. I'd had a bit going on.

Trish brought me the hands-free. "Hello Wayne, I only just got in from Hong Kong. Yes, I know, a terrible thing, and the very reason I'd been retained to prevent. No, I realise I shouldn't blame myself, but nevertheless, I don't feel great about it. Could you answer a question for me? What will now happen to her majority shareholding?"

"Well, we have a buy-sell agreement in place," Wayne explained, "which allows the company or other shareholders to buy back the shares from the estate of the deceased shareholder. This helps to ensure the company remains in the hands of the remaining shareholders and can continue to operate smoothly,"

"Thank you, Wayne. Who is taking care of the funerary arrangements?"

"I believe that'll be Dicky. I'll make sure you're on the A-list."

"Much obliged, Wayne."

"I expect now that you're relieved of your contract, you'll drop the case?"

"No, I have a sense of obligation to help the NYPD to solve it."

"I see. Just let me know if I can be of further assistance."

While on hands-free, I walked into my office. I flopped into the chair behind my desk and mulled over what Brown had said. With the company on the verge of going public, Charlotte's 51% stake was worth a king's ransom. I wondered what price they'd pay for the shares and who gets first dibs? It seemed to me that Mr Brown was firmly in charge. Should I consider him a suspect? It was time to phone Bulldog for his take.

"Hey, Dog, how goes it?"

"Back from the mysterious Orient? You guys have all the fun," he joked.

"It wasn't so pretty, three murders and a kidnapping, a bloody triad war over Charlie's inheritance."

"Jesus, what did he inherit, half of Hong Kong?"

"Almost, a nightclub, right in the guts of town, freehold and all, joint makes a million a month. Anyhow, enough of that, what's the story with my client Charlotte Austin now deceased?"

"Yeah, not doing your job very well there, buddy ... the prediction became reality."

"Don't rub it in. So, give me what you've got."

"Nothing, I've been waiting for you to give me the good oil on the family. Seems it's a sophisticated version of the Hatfield and the McCoy feud."

"You're not wrong. Who have you questioned?"

"The terrorist, Avalon, aka a crowd of names, the security of the apartment block ... you know it's the best address in Manhattan, right?"

"Sure do."

"So security provided Avalon an alibi. Spoke with the staff ... nothing ... the Doctor who found her in the pool, he's legit, tried to resuscitate her, thought she'd drowned ... well, she had, but she had enough poison in her to fell a horse. Autopsy shows the poison did the job even though the official certificate states death by drowning. Haven't started on the family or the company, like I said, I've been awaiting the emperor's return," he said light-heartedly.

"So no-one saw an entry, no sign in, nothing?"

"Got the CCTV footage of the lobby, elevator, and the floor, nothing ... but, we got something from the service elevator, I think it's the perp, face is obscured, but by the gait I'd put my house on it being a woman."

"Can you send me the best section of the CCTV?"

"Yep, done."

"What can I do?" I asked.

"Talk to the family and Valiant ... did you have a leading suspect for the letter before you left town, Kendy thought you did?"

"My money was originally on Avalon, but he turned out to be Charlotte's brother, as you know ... after interrogating him, I ruled him out. Now I'm betting on the disgruntled family members, specifically the Lincoln Austin, estranged oldest son of Charlotte's deceased husband, and/or his two children, both in their early twenties and spoilt to the max, Camille and Joseph Austin. The siblings don't get on, so there's value there to play them off against one another. I haven't interviewed Lincoln. Then there's Wayne Brown, CEO of Valiant, I spoke to him before I called you, he seems clean. Then there's Richard Wilks, the COO, he seems unlikely but hey, there's so much bread involved any one of them or all of them could be in it up to their eyebrows, they all stand to gain from her death—the only one that doesn't, is Avalon. Finally, there's the oldest son Dallas Austin, he has a chip on his shoulder the size of Nebraska, and was expected to succeed to the top but didn't, beaten there by Charlotte—so he's a possible candidate."

"Okay, how about you go talk to them all, narrow it down, you're across it ... it would take a detective a month of Sunday's to get to where you are now. Keep me posted. Can you get on it right away?"

"The emperor has returned, no worries, mate."

"Good, going to the concert tonight?"

"Yep, you?"

"Promised Kendy," Bulldog said, "see you there."

Patricia came in, "Aren't you tired, it was a long flight?"

"Slept all the way, come here." I helped her onto my lap and gave her a hug, she felt good in my arms. "I've missed you," I admitted. We kissed.

~ ~ ~

In a dimly lit warehouse on Argyle Street, Mong Kok, Hong Kong, two cars pulled up next to two others, their headlights cutting through the darkness. Four men, including Wing Lee of the Red Dragon, stepped out of the newly arrived cars.

From the parked cars, five men emerged, led by Da ye Zhu, a formidable enforcer of the Wo Shing Wo. He roughly dragged Wan Foon, the captured red pole of the Red Dragon, from one of the cars. Foon was gagged and bound, his face bruised and battered under the harsh light of the headlights.

A tense standoff unfolded as Wing Lee, flanked by his men, faced Zhu's crew. Zhu approached Wing with Foon in tow, then suddenly slashed the ties binding Foon's hands. Foon yanked down his gag and shouted a warning in Chinese, but it was too late.

Zhu retreated swiftly to his men as they brandished their weapons. The air erupted with gunfire as an Uzi submachine gun thundered from beneath a coat. Foon was the first to fall, riddled with bullets. Zhu then zeroed in on Wing, who was attempting to find cover. A single shot to the knee brought Wing down as the rest of the Red Dragon fell under the hail of gunfire. Only one of Zhu's men was hit in the chaos.

As the smoke cleared, the Red Dragon lay in a bloody heap, their bodies punctured with bullet holes. Zhu approached the wounded Wing, whose futile attempt to reach his gun ended inches short. Resigned, Wing looked up at Zhu. Zhu, without hesitation, emptied his clip into Wing's face, erasing his identity in a brutal final act.

Tan Fang, through Zhu's ruthless efficiency, had eliminated the unwanted partner and effectively decimated the Red Dragon's leadership. Zhu knelt beside Wing's body, revealing the skull and crossbones tattoo on his arm. He then methodically took photos of the tattoo and the grisly aftermath with his phone.

~ ~ ~

Charlie was lounging with Carmen by the pool at his Hollywood Hills home, basking in their recent successes, when his phone buzzed with a text. Opening the message, he was confronted with a ghastly photograph. The image made it clear why Tan Fang had readily accepted Wing Lee as a 30% partner. The brutality of the photo was stark, and Charlie reluctantly showed it to Carmen, who winced at the sight.

He forwarded the photo to Nick, me, and Zhong, then quickly typed a message to Michael Wong, instructing him to halt the transfer of shares. In the wake of recent events, Charlie decided to claim Wing Lee's 30%, restoring his father's full share in the business. He had no illusions about Fang, his 40% partner, and what he was capable of. The thought left Charlie uneasy, but he took some solace in having Zhong as a mediator for his interests.

Reflecting on Wing's fate, Charlie realised he felt no remorse. Wing's life, marred by violence and treachery, seemed almost fated to end in tragedy. He shared this unsettling revelation with Carmen, who gently took his hand, offering a comforting perspective. "Some things are just meant to be, darling."

In that moment, Charlie understood the complex web of fate and choice, feeling the weight of decisions made long ago and their repercussions in the present.

~ ~ ~

Receiving Charlie's photo, I couldn't help but shake my head at the stark reality of the situation. The extreme measures taken by Charlie's partner, Tan Fang, were unsettling, yet it was clear that this had been Fang's calculated plan from the start—a treacherous and cunning move. This reaffirmed my decision that having Zhong handle our Hong Kong operations was the right call.

Inspired by Agatha Christie, I decided to set up a meeting with Dallas, Lincoln, Camille, and Joe Austin, along with Wayne Brown and Richard Wilks, in the Valiant boardroom. The goal was to possibly unmask or at least get closer to identifying the true perpetrator behind the recent events. I tasked Patricia with organising this meeting, presenting it as an official police request to lend it legitimacy.

To cover all bases, I rang up Bulldog to brief him on this plan. It was crucial to ensure that if any of the Austin family or their associates called to confirm the meeting's validity, Bulldog would corroborate our story. He agreed that this was a prudent approach.

By the day's end, Patricia had successfully set up the meeting for 11 am the next day—ironically, Black Friday, the 13th. A fitting date for what I hoped would be a revealing gathering.

CHAPTER
FOURTEEN

rriving at Carnegie Hall, we caught the tail end of the support act, 'Velcro.' Their closing number, 'Stuck on You,' amusingly mirrored their name.

Our seats nestled us comfortably between Bulldog and the pair, Lucy Yip and Ren Tanaka. Before we could exchange pleasantries, the hall dimmed into an expectant darkness as 'Lunatic Fringe' began their set. A singular, intense spotlight bathed Rag Doll in its glow, reminiscent of that divine light which had enveloped Angel from outer space on the Lindos Resort pier. In this celestial spotlight, Rag Doll took on an almost angelic presence.

The thought crossed my mind that Kendy might have drawn inspiration for the lighting from the tale of God's door I had shared. The opening of 'I've Got Tomorrow' was mesmerising, featuring Slick's David Gilmour-esque slide guitar and Kendy's Richard Wright-style keyboards, conjuring a dreamlike, ethereal atmosphere.

As Rag Doll stood enveloped in that heavenly light, she suddenly locked her gaze with the audience, her voice soaring as she began to sing.

You
and I
Looking up

to the sky
Days
Go by
Oh how they fly
I wonder why
Only you
Know the answer
To the days
The days of my life.

Ooo, ooo, oo, can you hear me?
Ooo, ooo, oo, you're up there somewhere.
You know it's true
The big day is coming
And I know it too
There's no sense in running, in running
In running
Help,
please be kind
I've got tomorrow
On my mind

Ooo, ooo, oo can you hear me?
Ooo, ooo, oo you're up there somewhere.
You know it's true
The big day is coming
And I know it too
There's no sense in running, in running
In running,

Help, please be kind
I've got tomorrow
On my mind

Everybody has to think for tomorrow
Stop thinking about today
I've got tomorrow
On my mind

Help,
please be kind
I've got tomorrow
On my mind

Help,
please be kind
I've got tomorrow
On my mind

Help, help, help,
please be kind
I've got tomorrow
On my mind...

The concert was a resounding success, culminating in 'Fringe' delivering an encore with their hit 'Femme Fatale.' The crowd rose to their feet, swaying and dancing to the rhythm. As the applause echoed through Carnegie Hall, we prepared to head backstage, our passes ready.

Just as we neared the dressing room, a sudden tug from a shadowy alcove startled me. It was Rhett Avalon, pulling me aside urgently. I signalled for Patricia and Bulldog to continue without me.

"Rhett, you could get seriously hurt surprising people like that," I chastised him, noting his distressed look.

"I'm sorry ... I just ... I feel like I'm to blame for my sister's death. I was only gone for half an hour ... Someone knew my routine," he stammered, on the verge of tears.

"It's okay, Rhett. I know it wasn't you," I reassured him, trying to calm his nerves.

"I meet with Clarry daily to discuss security ... Charlotte was all the family I had, Axis. I never wanted any harm to come to her."

"Did the police know about your routine?"

"Yes, I told them."

"That means this was premeditated, Rhett. Probably involved more than one person," I speculated.

"But how did they bypass security?"

"We have CCTV footage of the suspect entering through the delivery bay and using the service elevator. They must have been familiar with the building's layout."

"Charlotte was so precise; everything in her life was like clockwork because of her OCD. The timing of the attack had to be perfect."

"That's an interesting point. Did the killer know her schedule? Is it posted online?"

"Yes, I update a weekly schedule every Monday, accessible only to the staff and Charlotte."

"We need to check those logs. Who else had the login details?" I asked.

"Just six staff members, myself, and Charlotte."

"No family members?"

"No."

"Alright, I need you to check the staff's employment history for any connections to the Austin family. I'll have Patricia look into the ISP logs. Send me the details."

"Okay, I'll handle it tonight. Thanks, Axis."

"Go relax, Rhett. We're on this. We'll find who's responsible."

After leaving Rhett, I re-joined Patricia and Bulldog in the dressing room.

True to his word, Rhett sent the necessary information, and by 9 am the next day, Patricia had a printout of the ISP activity. It didn't take us long to find the critical piece of evidence we needed. With the 11 am meeting at Valiant looming, we doubled down on our research, determined to piece together the final elements of this intricate puzzle.

~ ~ ~

Exiting the elevator on the 30th floor, I spotted Dallas Austin in the corridor. He cast a glance over his shoulder before signalling me to follow him into a small office opposite the boardroom.

The room was sparse, furnished with only a desk, a chair, and a small east-facing window. Austin, visibly agitated, confronted me. "Stone, listen and listen well. You weren't invited to probe into Charlotte's death. She hired you for a different task, which you failed. I don't appreciate being summoned here with my family and executives for your interrogation. Understand?"

I met his fury with equal intensity. "Back off, Austin," I countered sharply. "I don't take threats lightly, especially from a suit like you."

Austin recoiled, realising I wasn't to be intimidated. I pressed on, "Here's the deal: I'm not done until Charlotte's killer is found. This investigation is under NYPD jurisdiction. If you question its legitimacy, feel free to verify it with them. Holding this interview here is merely a courtesy, rather than downtown at the station. Your preference?"

He relented, "No."

"That's what I thought." My phone chimed with 'The Terrible Tango', signalling a text. Dismissing Austin, I turned and strode into the boardroom.

Austin brushed past me, taking his place among the other Austins. Across from them sat Brown and Wilks. The atmosphere in the room was heavy with tension. I remained standing, ready to confront the gathering storm of emotions and revelations that lay ahead.

"Good morning," I began with cordial professionalism. "Thank you all for attending. Today, we're here to discuss the events leading up to Charlotte Austin's murder."

Lincoln Austin interjected sceptically, "I fail to see the relevance to us, or you for that matter. You're a private detective, aren't you?"

"This meeting is sanctioned by the NYPD," I replied coolly. "I'm collaborating with them on this investigation. As for its relevance to you, Mr Austin, the person responsible for Mrs Austin's murder and the threatening notes predicting her death is among us in this room."

Murmurs of unease rippled through the gathered group. I let my statement hang in the air, allowing the tension to build. "The killer made several critical mistakes. Firstly, we have CCTV footage. While the face is obscured, other identifiers like height and gait are evident. The perpetrator needed intimate knowledge of Charlotte's schedule to poison her coffee. Yes, she was poisoned before drowning in her swimming pool."

Surprised glances shot around the room.

"Charlotte's OCD meant her life was meticulously scheduled. The perpetrator accessed this schedule from a private website. An accomplice was also needed to sneak into the apartment, bypass the maid, and poison the coffee. A well-timed phone call to the landline ensured the maid would be elsewhere when the deed was done. The CCTV captured the act taking just three minutes."

I then dropped the bombshell about the maid's connection to Lincoln Austin's household, causing Lincoln to bristle with indignation. Before he could protest, I redirected the accusation. "However, Mr. Lincoln Austin is not our murderer. That distinction goes to you, Miss Camille Austin."

I signalled Bulldog, who entered. "This is lieutenant Bixby from the NYPD. Lieutenant, any news from the maid, Thelma Reid?"

"She's provided enough to charge Miss Camille Austin with murder, and Mr Joe and Mr Lincoln Austin with conspiracy."

As the officers took them into custody, their calm demeanour surprised me. I expected more of a reaction, particularly from Camille.

Dallas Austin approached me. "My apologies for earlier, Mr Stone. You're quite the investigator."

"People often underestimate me, Mr Austin."

Wayne Brown congratulated me too. "Impressive work, Axis. Felt like a scene straight out of a Hercule Poirot novel."

"I did take a page from the great detective's book. By the way, I suggest hiring Charlotte's brother for your security team. He was instrumental in solving this, and with his sister gone he'll need a new position now."

"I'll consider your recommendation," Wayne assured.

With the case wrapped up, I felt a sense of accomplishment. It was a complex web of deception and betrayal, but justice had been served.

~ ~ ~

Back at the office, Kendy and Patricia were eagerly waiting for the lowdown on the case closure. As I began recounting the details, my phone buzzed with Charlie's name lighting up the screen. I excused myself and took the call in my office.

"Hey, Charlie. That photo you sent was pretty grim," I started.

"Yeah, I wouldn't want to be on Tan Fang's bad side. Got a call from Zhong—he's joining our firm. He's quite thrilled about it. And I heard from Wong; he hadn't transferred the shares to Wing. So, I'm still holding onto the 60%."

"Does that worry you?"

"Not at all. The income and capital gain from the property will be beneficial. Plus, I can afford to pay Zhong well to manage my interests in Utopia 8, Circle Three, and our operations at Cat Street."

"Seems like everything worked out in the end."

"Yeah, thanks to you and Nick. I really appreciate it, mate."

"That's what partners are for, Charlie."

"You say that, Axis, but you both put your necks on the line for me. I won't forget that."

"We know you'd do the same."

Then Charlie's tone shifted. "Speaking of which, I've got a new case on my hands. Thought you might be interested."

Stay tuned for the next gripping chapter in
the Axis Stone Mystery Series

Book Nine
'THE ZIGGY STARDUST DEAD RINGER'